SPECIAL MESSAGE TO READERS

This book is published under the auspices of

THE ULVERSCROFT FOUNDATION

(registered charity No. 264873 UK)

Established in 1972 to provide funds for research, diagnosis and treatment of eye diseases. Examples of contributions made are: —

A Children's Assessment Unit at Moorfield's Hospital, London.

•

Twin operating theatres at the Western Ophthalmic Hospital, London.

•

A Chair of Ophthalmology at the Royal Australian College of Ophthalmologists.

•

The Ulverscroft Children's Eye Unit at the Great Ormond Street Hospital For Sick Children, London.

You can help further the work of the Foundation by making a donation or leaving a legacy. Every contribution, no matter how small, is received with gratitude. Please write for details to:

**THE ULVERSCROFT FOUNDATION,
The Green, Bradgate Road, Anstey,
Leicester LE7 7FU, England.
Telephone: (0116) 236 4325**

**In Australia write to:
THE ULVERSCROFT FOUNDATION,
c/o The Royal Australian and New Zealand
College of Ophthalmologists,
94-98 Chalmers Street, Surry Hills,
N.S.W. 2010, Australia**

DURANGO GUNHAWK

They called him the Durango Gunhawk after he out-drew and out-shot four vengeful pursuers in the town of Durango. Many followed, wanting the title of fastest gun in the West. It was hard just staying alive — he attracted trouble. So when he was hoping to pass through Killdeer Valley, out came the guns of the backshooters and those with old scores to settle. Durango wished he had given Killdeer Valley a wide berth — run or stay, he'd have to fight.

Books by Tyler Hatch
in the Linford Western Library:

A LAND TO DIE FOR
BUCKSKIN GIRL
DEATHWATCH TRAIL
LONG SHOT
VIGILANTE MARSHAL
FIVE GRAVES WEST
BIG BAD RIVER
CHEYENNE GALLOWS
DEAD WHERE YOU STAND!

TYLER HATCH

DURANGO GUNHAWK

Complete and Unabridged

LINFORD
Leicester

First published in Great Britain in 2007 by
Robert Hale Limited
London

First Linford Edition
published 2008
by arrangement with
Robert Hale Limited
London

British Library CIP Data

Hatch, Tyler
Durango Gunhawk.—Large print ed.—
Linford western library
1. Western stories
2. Large type books
I. Title
823.9′2 [F]

ISBN 978–1–84782–090–7

Published by
F. A. Thorpe (Publishing)
Anstey, Leicestershire

Set by Words & Graphics Ltd.
Anstey, Leicestershire
Printed and bound in Great Britain by
T. J. International Ltd., Padstow, Cornwall

This book is printed on acid-free paper

1

THE RIDER

'Hey!' The sheriff paused, waiting for the rider to turn and acknowledge his call.

But the man on the buckskin kept walking the mount down the busy main drag of Two Rivers.

'Hey! You on the buckskin!'

Sheriff Link Waterman stepped out of his office doorway onto the landing in front of the law office. He was middle-aged, tough-looking, dressed tolerably well for a frontier lawman, wearing twin sixguns in studded holsters on a buscadero rig. And he had a short fuse.

This time the rider turned his head but the horse kept going at its slow walking pace. The animal showed signs of long, hard travel, its stride weary, but firm enough, good long muscles showing beneath the dusty hide.

'Yeah, you! You deaf?'

The rider was slumped over a little but he would ride tall when he straightened, and his shoulders were square and high, his upper body long, legs the same. Here was a big man in trail-stained clothes, wearing a single Colt in a weathered holster, polished, but from long use it seemed to the lawman rather than with applied oil. The man turned his head slowly and although the curl-brim of his hat shadowed his features some, Waterman could see they were lean, stubbled, with eyes that looked indifferent even from this distance.

The man didn't answer the sheriff, kept his horse walking.

'Come here! I want a word with you.'

The man turned front again, the buckskin still walking. Waterman swore under his breath, was aware of folk on the street slowing now, sensing some sort of confrontation here. He dropped his right hand to his Colt's butt.

'Mister! I said I want a word with you!'

'On my way back, Sheriff,' a deep voice told him, the man not looking at him now. 'Horse is kinda tuckered — like its rider. I'll get him stabled then come see you.'

'You'll damn well come see me *now!*' Waterman was angry that he had to shout, trying to lend extra authority to his words, as if the glinting tin star on his frayed edged vest wasn't enough.

The man just shook his head. 'This is a good horse — I'll see him cared for, dip my head in a bucket of water and be back — ten minutes, no more.'

Waterman's clean-shaven jaw jutted and his mouth tightened. He tried not to see the curious, expectant faces of the townsfolk watching. Then he abruptly pulled his watch from a vest pocket, flipped the cover open.

'I got the clock on you, mister!'

The rider lifted a hand languidly and eased towards the big open doors of the livery stables beyond a rail fence with an open, sagging gate.

Waterman stood impatiently on his landing, glancing at his watch every few seconds. There was a small crowd gathering across the street and he cursed inwardly. *This ranny, whoever he was, was gonna be damn sorry he put him through this! Challenging his authority.*

He felt the anger seething and he began to feel the hardening of a cold knot in his belly as the watch hands crept up to the ten-minute mark — and passed it. He sucked in a deep breath, frowning as he glanced at the livery doors. No sign of the big rider!

He rammed the watch back into his vest so hard he tore the small pocket's stitching. Then, loosening both guns in their holsters, he strode to the steps leading down to the street. He had reached the bottom one when the stranger appeared, walking with easy stride through the gateway of the livery, carrying a warbag in one hand, a rifle in the other. For a moment, it looked like he was going to turn away from the law office, but he was only checking for traffic as a big, laden Conestoga rumbled by, screening him briefly.

Link Waterman waited, tensed. *If he had to go after this son of a bitch . . .*

But the man was crossing the street now, came right over and stood a yard from the waiting sheriff.

'You're late!' the lawman snapped, aware that it sounded more like a carping complaint than a reprimand.

'Had to wake the hostler.'

The man waited and Waterman looked him over, feeling only a slight easing of that cold knot in his belly.

'You must've come over the bridge,' Waterman said abruptly, pointing back briefly the way the rider had come. The man nodded slightly. 'Then you should've seen the sign that says all arrivals report first to my law office — or can't you read?'

'I can get by. I'm here, Sheriff. What's the problem?'

'Who said there was a problem? It's an order I've placed at both sides of town and I expect drifters like you to obey it.'

The big man said nothing, his face expressionless. The sheriff didn't like being forced to wait out a reply that never came, made him do the explaining.

'I've got enough troubles without gunslingers drifting in here, lookin' to make a fast buck.'

Still the newcomer waited and the sheriff felt his face darkening. 'Goddammit! What's your name?'

'I'm called Durango.'

'I ain't interested in nicknames! I want your real name.'

'Only name I go by.'

There was no fear in this man: neither the badge nor the twin guns seemed to bother him. But his manner bothered Waterman: he had a bad feeling about this stranger.

'Durango, huh? Come from there, the town, or down Mexico way?'

'Not Mexico and it's not my home town. Was only there once.'

'How come they call you Durango then?'

The man looked levelly at the sheriff, both men of about the same height — six feet, maybe an inch or so more, but Durango was heavier and more solid than the lawman.

He sighed. 'I can see you're gonna worry at this like a dog, Sheriff — Durango was where I got into some trouble.'

Link Waterman narrowed his eyes, dropped them to the man's single sixgun, noting the wear on the holster and the hand-polished cedar butt again. 'You kill a man?'

Durango hesitated. 'Four.'

Waterman jolted, blinked despite himself. 'The hell you say!'

'They were the father, two brothers and a brother-in-law of some cocky kid who got drunk in Laredo and pushed me into a gunfight.'

'And you killed him! You must push

easy, feller, if some kid can make you draw, or were you hunting a rep?'

Durango kept that steady gaze on the man's face. 'Maybe I already had the rep along the Border.'

Waterman nodded gently. 'Uh-huh. Now we're gettin' someplace.' He suddenly shook a stiffened forefinger in Durango's face. 'Now you listen good, mister — the reason for them signs about reportin' to me is because I don't want gunslingers in my town, nor even my county! Now, I dunno which one of the valley ranchers sent for you, but you just climb aboard that buckskin of yours when he's tended to and keep ridin'. You hear?'

'No one sent for me.'

'The hell you say! Look, there's been trouble out in the valley for months. Coupla men've been killed, others have been run off — or carried off. Them big ranchers think they can do what they like but I'm damned if they will, so you just get outa my bailiwick, Durango, and keep ridin'.'

'My business here won't take long.'

The sheriff stiffened. 'Are you dumb? I just told you, you ain't stayin'! Not for another half-hour even! If you think — '

The words suddenly stopped. The rifle had swung up casually in Durango's hand: it could have been deliberate, or it may have just moved when Durango dropped his warbag to the dusty street and thumbed back his hat.

'Sheriff, I'm not interested in your troubles — I've got me a little business here and I aim to do it, then ride on. I'm not looking for any kinda trouble.'

Waterman ran a tongue around his suddenly dry lips. 'Point that rifle someplace else! *Now!*'

Durango looked down at the Winchester, arched dark eyebrows. 'This rifle? I'm just holding it, Sheriff. I'm not menacing you or anyone else with it. But . . . ' He let the barrel sag a few inches: his grip on the stock didn't change, and his finger was still through the trigger guard, a thumb resting in the curve of the hammer spur.

Suddenly Waterman paled. 'Jesus! I know who you are now! Shoulda figured when you mentioned them four you killed — the Clayton boys, and the old man, Todd Clayton! Meanest sons of bitches ever rode the Rio!'

Slowly Durango nodded. 'It was the Claytons, and their in-law, Buster Haymes.'

'I s'pose you were pushed into that gunfight, too!'

'Told you why they braced me.'

'Yeah — and you came outa there known as the Durango Gunhawk! Hell, that must be — what? Five years ago?'

'About — it don't matter, Sheriff. I'm not in your town looking for trouble. That makes three, four times I've told you now.'

'No, you been paid to look for it out in the valley! Who they want you to run off? The small-timers? One of the spreads Big John Dancey's havin' trouble with?'

'I don't know any Dancey or anyone else around here, Sheriff. I don't aim to stick around after I finish my business.'

'Just what is your damn business here?'

'Mine.'

'By God, you're a sassy one, ain't you? Don't think your rep means anythin' to me! This is my town, my valley — and I say who stays and who don't.'

'Sounds to me like this Dancey and his pards have a say in things, too.'

Waterman's lips were razor thin. 'I don't care how it seems to you! And you shouldn't, neither, 'cause you *ain't stayin'!* Now, how many times I gotta say that?'

'About as many as I say I'll leave when I finish my business here.'

The sheriff was fighting a tremble going right through his body now. He had been aware of townsfolk edging closer so as to better hear what was going on. It enraged him to be caught back on his heels this way. But he knew he had correctly identified this rider now and he knew blamed well he was no match for the Durango Gunhawk.

Maybe if he hadn't been so stubborn — *all right, downright greedy!* — and hired some deputies out of his pay. But he was alone here. Had enjoyed running things his way *and* was tough enough to do it! Well, he had no back-up now and he knew the townsmen wouldn't give him any: his arrogance and bullying of the citizens had been tolerated because the town liked the streets to be free of gunfights and even brawls. But he had told everyone so many times that he could — and *would* — run things his way that now, if he tried to hire deputies, they would laugh in his face, tell him to go ahead and sort it out himself. That's the way he did things, wasn't it? Or — couldn't he handle this stranger . . . ?

'You say you ain't here to use your gun?' he said abruptly, annoyed he had to pause and clear his throat. Durango nodded. 'That gospel?'

'I said it.'

Waterman nodded jerkily, smarting

under the murmur of the townsfolk now gathered along the boardwalk and in the street itself.

'All right, you got twenty-four hours. Then you not only clear the valley, you get right outa my county.'

Durango nodded slowly. 'That ought to be long enough.'

'It damn well *will* be!' Waterman rode it for all it was worth now the man looked like accepting the deadline.

'We'll see. You recommend a good rooming-house, Sheriff? One with a bath facility?'

Waterman, a petty man at times, snorted, waved a hand vaguely. 'Go look for yourself — I've wasted enough time on you.'

Durango lifted his warbag and, still holding his rifle ready to shoot if necessary, started walking, looking at the faded signs on falsefronts as the crowd opened out.

2

FEAR

Big John Dancey placed one foot on the bottom rail of the corral and watched some of his crew branding the calves they had brought in from the south pasture the previous night.

'Burn it in deep!' he called, as one of the men seemed to barely touch the hot iron to the red hide. 'I don't want it so shallow some son of a bitch can change it with a runnin' iron.'

The cowboy made acknowledgement to the order and settled the iron on the next hide, leaning his weight on it. Dancey was about to yell at the man he didn't want the damn calf barbecued, either, when he became aware of a galloping horse. He turned his big, shaggy head, the yellow locks with a few iron-grey streaks falling across his ice-blue eyes. Irritably he pushed the strands aside, saw a rider skidding to a halt in a cloud of dust, recognizing his foreman, Arlo Jeffries, who had been sent to town earlier for round-up supplies. The rancher looked past him but didn't see the loaded buck-board that ought to be following just behind Jeffries.

'What the hell, Arlo? Where's Max?'

Jeffries, a gangling man, lean and hard, tossed his rein ends over the head of his sweating horse and hurried across. He jerked a thumb vaguely over his shoulder.

'He'll be here later, Boss. Been heavy floodin' upstream and the supply wagon was late; I rode on ahead, figured you'd want to hear.' He paused but the rancher remained silent, impatient. 'There's a gunfighter in town, too! Faced down Waterman and made him eat crow!'

Both items were of interest to Dancey: Waterman eating crow was something to think about, and the fact there was a gunfighter in Two Rivers.

'I never sent for no gunfighter. Was thinking on it but — who the hell's he here to see?'

'Dunno. Wouldn't say. Sheriff put the clock on him, give him twenty-four hours to do his business. Feller just, cool as you like, told the sheriff the time *might* be enough for him, but if it wasn't, he'd finish his business then ride on.'

Dancey frowned. 'Waterman stood still for that?'

'Din' have much choice. This Durango just walked off and the sheriff was too buffaloed to stop him.'

'Durango?' Dancey's gaze sharpened. 'Not that Durango Gunhawk *hombre*?'

'Yeah. That's the one.'

Dancey frowned deeper, shook his head slowly. 'Now who in hell would go and hire him? Has to be someone from the alliance — none of them ham-'n'-egger spreads could afford him, not even if they pooled their money.'

'Just thought you'd want to know, boss.'

'Yeah, yeah, OK, Arlo. Go help yourself to a drink of my whiskey. Oh, saddle me a horse first. The roan — I got some riding to do.'

'Checkin'-up on the alliance?' Arlo knew he had said too much. Dancey didn't care for his employees to be on too familiar terms with him and his business with the alliance, the small, tight group formed by the bigger cattle spreads in Killdeer Valley to make sure they retained every foot of what they termed 'free range' — free to them, no one else.

'Get that damn roan saddled,' the rancher growled, his eyes cold and hard now. 'You won't have time for that drink, come to think of it. Soon as Max gets here, start unloading the buckboard and get them stores catalogued. I've had enough of missing cans and bottles and such from the storehouse shelves. You make sure the door's padlocked, too.'

Arlo Jeffries cursed himself for being too talkative and nodded, taking his lariat from the pommel of his blowing horse and moving to the small remuda corral.

He hoped Dancey wouldn't find out who had sent for Durango until it was too late. *Well, hell, no, he didn't really mean that! But Dancey sure could rile a man without half trying. He was getting tired of this job, anyway . . .*

Ten minutes later, Big John Dancey spurred his roan out of the yard, slipping a loaded Winchester into the saddle scabbard first. Arlo noticed he had also strapped on a sixgun.

Looked like things were going to be humming in the valley pretty soon. Just wait till the fear started to spread if Dancey couldn't find out who had sent for Durango! Man, there'd be a line-up at every privy in the damn valley with folk stirring old misdeeds in their consciences.

Then Arlo suddenly remembered a woman in Brownsville, all those years ago, back in his bad days. Her crippled brother had sworn he would get him someday. His last words suddenly rang through Arlo Jefferies' head:

'*She cared for me and now I got no one — I mightn't be able to come after you myself, but I can send someone. You can look over your shoulder for the rest of your life and one day, he'll be there. With your name on a bullet!*'

Judas! Arlo broke out in a sweat now just thinking about it. He'd changed his name but — could that kid still be trying to square things?

He glanced in the direction Dancey had ridden. Just a cloud of dust now, couldn't even see the horse.

'Miserable sounver'll never know whether I took a drink of his whiskey or not! And I could sure use one now!'

Mopping his face, he hurried into the house, making quietly for Dancey's office.

* * *

Brant Collier of B Bar C was Dancey's first call. He was owner of the next biggest spread to Dancey's Circle D — and a man who had a deal of money he could lay his hands on. Not in any bank, but . . . somewhere. He could always come up with a fistful of dollars when needed. *Tight as a fish's ass, though*.

Collier was fortyish, a medium tall man, weighed about 175 pounds and wore his hair close-cropped, his scalp showing a lot of scaly flakes that he swore were something more than dandruff and needed a special unguent rubbed in each night. He scratched at his scalp above his right ear now as Dancey told him about the arrival of the gunhawk from Durango. Collier's round face didn't change expression but his heavy frontier moustache twitched.

'No use lookin' at me, John. I might've sent for him if I'd thought of it, but I'd've put it to the alliance first, you know that.'

'I guess you would — to spread the cost!' Dancey said crisply. He seemed edgy. 'Must be pretty tough. According to Arlo, he buffaloed Waterman and that hardhead don't buffalo easy. Too dumb to back down.'

Collier frowned. 'Think Case'd do it without tellin' us?'

'He better not have! No, no, Case is like me: got too many damn expenses right now. He'd never go it alone. He'd want to make sure everyone paid his share.'

'He come expensive, this gunhawk?'

'So I hear. Damn! I hate this kinda thing, something happening in the valley outside of our control.'

'What about Shaw and the other nesters?'

Dancey looked at Collier sharply and smiled crookedly. 'You're loco, Brant. Them homesteaders couldn't rake up enough between 'em to keep Durango in tobacco. No, it's someone with money — and outside of the alliance. I dunno who the hell it could be. But I don't like it!'

Collier pursed his lips. 'We better

find out.' Then, as he had another thought he stroked his moustache. 'Could Durango be here for some other reason?'

'Like what?'

'Well, anyone can hire him, I guess. Just because he's here in Killdeer Valley don't mean for sure it's anythin' to do with us.'

Dancey's face was suddenly tight. 'You mean the alliance and the free range? You think it could be some other deal? Maybe some personal thing someone's hired him to settle for them?'

'Yeah. I guess most everyone's got somethin' in their past that — '

'You're riding the wrong trail, Brant,' Dancey cut in sharply. His ice-blue eyes were steady on the other's round face. '*I* ain't got anything to worry about that way, have you?'

Collier held the gaze, then looked away, shaking his head. ''Course not — it was just a thought. But, fact remains, Durango's here for somethin' and it's damn worryin'.'

'Yeah, well, it'd be too much of a coincidence the way things are here right now. No, it's something to do with our troubles and I aim to find out who Durango's working for . . . I'll go see Case, then — well, I guess we'll just have to keep an eye on Durango.'

'Who you have in mind?' Collier asked tautly.

'Arlo can do it: he was Waterman's deputy once. Getting too sassy, anyway. Needs something to pull him into line. A bit of boredom'll do him good.'

Brant Collier smiled, not warmly, more amused. 'You're a hard man, Big John.'

'You ain't seen nothing yet.' He finished the whiskey he was sharing with the other rancher and stood, running a hand through his long wavy blond hair before jamming his hat on. 'I'll go have a word with Case.'

'Gonna be kinda uncomfortable, not knowin' if this gunhawk *is* after our hides or not. Be nice if someone stopped him in his tracks.'

Dancey snorted. 'You find me the man who can out-draw him — even just *match* his draw — and I'll pay him five thousand dollars and give him a job for life.'

Collier's smile was twisted. 'Only thing is, a man that fast wouldn't live for long — someone faster'd come along. They always do . . . '

To Dancey, it seemed there was a touch of nostalgia or something akin to it in Brant Collier's words.

* * *

Durango decided it was too late to ride out into the valley today. By the time he'd visited the barber for a shave and haircut, taken a long soaking bath, bought himself some new shirts and a spare set of whipcord trousers, it was close to sundown.

Looking quite spruced up now, he tossed his room key onto the clerk's desk in the foyer of the Two Rivers

Hotel and asked, 'Where's a good place to eat?'

'Bijou, mister, right down the street to your left — block and a half,' the clerk told him, hanging the keyring on a nail beneath the number 11.

Durango nodded, went out of the foyer. As he did, a man in range clothes who had been reading an old *Harper's Weekly*, set the magazine down and adjusted his black hat as he went out, glancing briefly at the wall board where keys to Number 11 still swung slightly.

* * *

Durango enjoyed the meal well enough although he'd eaten better in a score of towns. But his hunger was satisfied and that suited him: he wasn't a man who fussed over his grub.

He went into a general store, bought a slim cardboard packet of cigarillos and lit one before going outside again, snapping the match into flame on a horny thumbnail. From long habit, under cover of shaking out the match, he checked the street to right and left, and the dark maws of a couple of alleys just beyond the reach of oil lamps burning outside places of business.

It was a balmy evening and there were several people strolling the walks. A saloon echoed with some slightly slurred lyrics of an off-colour trail ditty and he smiled faintly. *Long time since he had heard that one — long time since he'd ridden with a trail herd . . .*

Well, all that was changed now, thanks to an argument over cards in a dump of a trail town whose name he'd almost, but not quite, forgotten: Dogleg Bend, within sight of a bend of the Mississippi and the riverboats. One of the men he was playing cards with had accused him of dealing off the bottom of the deck. He was surprised at how fast the others scattered and drinkers in the bar backed off quickly.

He figured the man who had called him a cheat must be known for this kind of behaviour — when he was losing and a stranger was an easy target. He saw right away how the man pushed back the tails of his coat so as to allow him fast access to his sixgun which was worn halfway down his thigh, the holster base tied down with a leather thong.

He still remembered that sick feeling that knotted his belly as he realized he was facing a pro gunfighter.

He swallowed, thought about backing down but something inside him wouldn't allow it. If he had to die defending his honour, then that's the way it was going to be.

'I hate card cheats!' the gambler-gunfighter said, and it was plain to see he was enjoying this, anticipating killing this greenhorn.

Durango — using his real name at that time — heard himself retort, 'Like I hate playing against sore losers who figure the best way out is to bully some easy-going trailhand who's had a run of luck.'

'That how you see it?' the gambler

asked, really amused now. '*Easy-goin*'? Actually, I think you could be right, wrangler, easy-goin' to Hell!'

And his hand flashed in a pale blur as he lifted his Colt from the tied-down holster and snapped it up into line, thumb notching back the hammer . . .

Then the amusement changed to amazement as, for a fraction of a second, he stared down the steady muzzle of Durango's pistol, saw the flame stab towards him —

That single shot had taken the gambler high in the chest, a few inches below the throat. It caught him at a point of balance where the impact picked him clear off the floor and hurled him back across another vacant table, crashing down in a tangle of splintering chairs.

The saloon was silent, though ears still rang with the echoes of that single shot . . . now, almost ten years later down the trail, Durango could still recall that sound.

A split second of violence and it

changed his entire life.

The man he had killed was known as Slip Hardesty, a gunfighter who had left dead men behind him in saloons and along the trails, at mining camps and in muddy streets from Deadwood to El Paso.

He was a gunfighter when he walked out of that saloon, whether he wanted to be or not. And it was less than a week later, when he was having a quiet drink in a bar in some two-men-and-a-dog town, when the local flashy crashed through the batwings, yelling, 'How about it, gunfighter?' and went for his twin guns even as he spoke.

Durango's reputation went up several notches when, caught off-guard, he still swept up his gun and nailed the challenger between the eyes. *Hell, he hadn't even aimed, just drew and fired, driven by a powerful instinct for self-preservation*.

That was how it started and how it continued and then someone offered to hire his gun in a range war and pay mighty good money. He figured if his chief talent was being able to shoot straight and fast, why the hell not rent out those talents? A man had to live — though for how long going down this particular trail he found himself on was anybody's guess. *Gun for hire. Ask for top dollar and, surprisingly, he got it*.

Then, eventually, came the fracas at Durango and the word was out: the Durango Gunhawk's reputation had sky-rocketed. He was the fastest gun alive and he could be hired — *not bought* — for top dollar.

Now here he was, and just his appearance in this average-looking Wyoming trail town had people giving him a wide berth and throwing that hard-nosed sheriff into a tizzy.

'*The price of fame, amigo*,' he told himself with a half-smile and stepped down off the walk as he crossed the mouth of a dark alley, drawing on his cigarillo.

Over the years, his instincts and senses had, of necessity, been honed about as finely as a human being's could be. And just as well . . .

He heard the faint click of a metal spring snapping a gun hammer back to full cock and instantly went down to one knee, right hand sweeping his Colt out of the worn leather holster, sharp eyes sensing rather than actually seeing a movement of darkness against slightly paler darkness.

The two shots blended and the gunflashes showed him a man crouched beside some old beer kegs. As the man half rose, staggering, his pistol twisting around his trigger finger, causing the gun to fire again, Durango saw the second man lit by this powderfiash, and snapped a shot at him.

It came too fast and he heard the bullet whine off one of the iron bands holding the barrel staves. Then came the sound of running boots going towards the back of the alley. Behind him in the street, people were yelling and running for cover.

Durango went down the alley after

the second assassin, sliding along the wall of a building. He tripped once, and his target also fell over something and there was a brief curse. Durango lunged to the far side of the alley. A gun triggered two fast shots out there in the vacant lot, nicely locating the quarry for him.

As the man spun and the flash faded, Durango brought him down and the body fell loosely. He ran forward, hammer spur under his thumb, trigger depressed, powder-smoke rasping his nostrils, ears ringing with the gunfire.

He almost fell over the body and, as he knelt, a rough voice he recognized said, behind him, 'Just stay down like that, gunfighter! You got a cocked scattergun pointed right between your shoulders. And it would sure pleasure me to use it!'

Sheriff Link Waterman.

3

KILLER ON THE LOOSE

'I knew you were trouble, moment I saw you ride in!'

Sheriff Waterman gritted the words between his teeth as he walked behind his desk, laid the sawn-off shotgun and Durango's Colt on the desk and turned up the oil lamp. He gestured curtly to a hard, straightback chair opposite as he dropped into his own swivel desk chair.

As Durango sat down easily, Waterman rammed his elbows on the desktop and cradled his chin in his hands, glaring.

'You reckon someone took a potshot at you from the alley.'

'It was an ambush.'

'So you killed the man who shot at you, then charged in and *gave chase* to a second man who might or might not have had anything to do with the first one and killed him, too.'

Durango shrugged. 'Was I supposed to stand there with the lights of Main behind me and let him keep shooting till he hit me?'

The sheriff waved a finger across the desk. 'Don't sass me, feller! You're a hair from bein' locked up and charged with murder.'

'You don't look particularly stupid, Waterman, but you sure act it.'

The lawman's nostrils flared and he moved tensely in his chair, leaning forward. 'By God! I damn well will lock you up!'

He reached for the shotgun and then sat back with a quick intake of breath as Durango moved so fast he seemed to blur as he snatched up his Colt off the desk, cocked it and held the barrel a few inches from the sheriff's pale face. Link's eyes lifted slowly and his breathing was audible as he eased himself slowly back into his chair.

'Now who's being stupid!' he managed to grind out.

Durango stared at him for a long minute, then lowered the gun hammmer and holstered the weapon as he sat down again. 'Just taking what's mine, Sheriff. Relax, can't you? I was walking along the street, minding my own business when someone started shooting at me from the alley — There were several people on the walks ahead and behind me. They'll have seen what happened. Why don't you go find them and ask?'

'I don't need you to tell me my job!'

'Well, I dunno about that — you're talking about locking me up, when I was the victim.'

'You're forgetting the two men you killed — I'd call them victims of somethin'!'

'Self-defence — and you're not going to be able to prove otherwise, Sheriff, much as you'd like to.'

Waterman glared, tapping his fingers in a drumming sound against his desk edge. 'You're damn sure of yourself, Durango! Might work with some lawmen, but it won't work with me. See, I ain't afraid of you or your reputation.'

'Well, why don't we leave it right there, Sheriff? Before I have to prove that you ought to be leery of me?' When the lawman frowned, stuck for an answer, the gunfighter said, quietly, 'Your memory good enough to recall how I picked up my Colt off your desk? One breath, Waterman, you were just one breath away from Boot Hill.'

The sheriff swallowed, still not speaking.

'Hell! I didn't come here for trouble.'

'It sure as hell follows you around, though!'

'That gunplay wasn't of my making.'

Waterman snorted. 'Just you comin' here caused it, damn you! Everyone knows you're here because someone hired your gun — and that means someone else is gonna die in my bailiwick!'

'They're wrong, and so're you. Told you before, no one here hired me.'

Waterman sighed exasperatedly. 'Then what the hell're you doin' in my town?'

'My business is out in Killdeer Valley. I just stopped over to have a bath and a decent meal and to sleep in a soft bed. I'll be out of your hair tomorrow.'

The sheriff looked slightly sceptical, but then decided to push what he saw as an advantage. 'All right. But you better be or you and me're goin' to go head to head!'

Durango smiled thinly, stood slowly. 'I don't think so, Sheriff. I really don't think so.'

'You better not stick around to find out!'

Shaking his head slowly, amused, Durango walked to the street door, letting the lawman have the last word.

There were folk hanging around outside the law office, some crowding the door, hoping to hear what was said inside, others looking at the two dead men slumped on the boardwalk where they had been propped up. They went silent and opened out as Durango appeared.

He took a lantern from the hand of one townsman, held it close to the dead faces. A woman gasped and turned away at the sight of the bloody wounds. 'Anyone know 'em?'

No one answered at first, and then one man he'd seen in the livery earlier cleared his throat and said, 'The one in the black hat is Tom Nye: mean cuss, been in a lot of trouble round here.'

There were murmurings of agreement and another man spoke up, pointing to the second corpse. 'That's Perry Tooth — got a place back in the hills beyond the valley. They say he killed a coupla homesteaders last year.'

Durango thanked the men and glanced up at Waterman standing in the doorway. 'Someone knew who to hire, Sheriff.'

'You be gone from town after breakfast,' Waterman snapped, seizing the opportunity to save face with the townsfolk.

Durango set down the lantern and moved away down the boardwalk towards the hotel.

He wasn't shaken any by the attempt on his life: there had been too many for him to show much reaction other than shooting down the would-be killers. But it was getting to be a damn nuisance lately, not being able to travel without someone trying to put a bullet in him. It used to be some cocky kid wanting to try to outdraw him. Now, it seemed he was a target for bushwhackers, too.

Just because someone figured he must have been hired to come and kill someone around these parts . . . As if death had to follow automatically once he appeared. We-ell . . . *let's not go into that too deep!*

Turning into the hotel and crossing the foyer to pick up his key at the desk, he smiled crookedly.

They were right, of course. Death was his constant companion. And he was getting damned tired of it.

Wearily, he started up the stairs to his

room. He paused at the door with his key ready to insert in the lock. There was no light showing under his door but he could smell hot oil — as if a burning lamp had just been extinguished and the fumes remained. Even as he thought about it, his Colt slid into his hand and he cocked the hammer slowly and silently.

Standing to one side, flat against the wall, he reached out with his left hand and turned the key, then the handle, and under the pressure of his stretched fingers the door swung inwards. He waited, expecting a shot, but nothing happened.

Durango didn't move, tensed, but patient. A minute passed — two — three. Then just as he was about to move and step swiftly through the doorway, a voice said from inside, 'C'mon, cowboy! I'll fall asleep in a minute!'

He froze. It was a woman's voice, sultry, inviting even with such mundane words spoken. There was enough huskiness there to infer what might happen if she *didn't* fall asleep right away.

He hadn't sent for a whore.

After a pause he stepped inside, swiftly, no more than a shadow melting into the darkness of the room to one side of the open door. He reached out a foot and kicked it closed. He heard her gasp at the thud, and then a deep-throated laugh.

'Well, they did say you were cautious! But I ain't gonna try and get away!'

'Who said?' he asked, and dropped to one knee.

Then he saw a book or some other small obstruction removed and he glimpsed a table lamp with a tiny flame burning in the smudged glass chimney, turned all the way down. He stretched out quickly on the floor even as she turned the flame up and amber light flooded the room.

Durango felt kind of foolish, lying there on the worn carpet with a cocked sixgun in hand, blinking in the wash of light. Then a tousled red head appeared over the side of the bed and a smiling face looked down at him, bare shoulders showing where the bedsheet slanted across, lots of hair spilling over the laughing features.

'I'd rather do it in a soft bed than on the floor but — no accounting for tastes, I guess.'

She flung back the sheet and swung bare, ivory-coloured legs to the floor, reaching her arms towards him as she dropped to her knees, naked as the gun glinting in his hand.

'Now wait a minute!' He started to scramble up, but smooth warm arms went around his neck and that mighty interesting sinewy body pressed him back against the wall. He felt her hitch herself a little, pushing her bosom towards his face — and between her arm and the side of one breast, he saw the curtain on the corner clothes closet move and a man in a plain grey shirt and with a wide-brimmed hat stepped out, lifting a sawn-off shotgun.

Durango wrenched violently, bringing a startled cry from the woman as he flung her down, threw himself across her body and angled his Colt up, triggering twice. The assassin was just bringing up the shotgun, thumbing the hammers, when the lead took him in the neck and through the middle of his chest. He was dead even before he began to fall and the gunfighter pushed the now yelling woman under the bed. The shotgun fell and one barrel exploded, shredding the mattress and window curtains with a charge of double-0 buckshot.

Then she started to scream and he couldn't shut her up until he slapped her across the face and the shock made her gasp, froze any further screams. By then the room was filling with other hotel guests and Sheriff Waterman pushed his way through roughly, carrying his own shotgun. He raked his cold gaze around, let it linger a little on the naked woman as she tried to drag the shot-riddled sheet across her white body. Some of the men crowding in the doorway nudged each other and opened their eyes wide.

'By *God*, Durango! Can't you do one goddamn thing without killin' someone!'

Durango had the woman by the arm now, dragged her past the angry lawman and pointed to the dead man and the smoking shotgun. He shook her, the red hair flying.

'See that shotgun? He was gonna use it — on both of us!'

Shocked, she shook her head vigorously. 'No! He wouldn't've!'

He leant down and yelled in her ear. '*Yes, dammit!* He didn't aim to let you live and tell who hired you to wait in my bed to distract me while he stepped out of the clothes closet.'

'You sayin' that . . . ?' began Waterman but Durango didn't even look at him.

He shook the terrified woman again, her hair flying, making a brief blaze like a wind-blown flame as the lamplight shone through it. 'You're still alive because I kept you that way, Red! You owe me! Who was it hired you to come up here and climb into my bed?'

'Listen, you, I'll ask the questions . . . ' Again the sheriff's words drifted off into nothing as he met the icy glare of Durango's eyes.

He frowned, started to speak, but the girl said, a distinct sob in her shaky voice, 'H-he did!' She pointed to the dead man. 'He — he said you were shy of women! Wanted me to — to help you get over it . . . while he . . . watched.' She stopped swallowing. 'I know some others in this town and . . . an' other places like to watch, an' I — '

'How much did he pay?' snapped Waterman.

'A-a hundred dollars . . . '

While the whistles and murmurs riffled through the crowd at such an amount, Durango said, 'He'd have collected it again after he killed you. You know him?'

She hesitated. The sheriff scowled.

'He's a drifter — works the valley spreads sometimes at round-up or brandin'. Name's Carey. A no-account.'

Some of the other men nodded or murmured agreement. The sheriff almost smiled as he looked at the gunfighter.

'Someone around here don't much care for you, Durango.'

'Ain't that the truth,' Durango agreed. 'Or maybe just by being here I scared up a bad conscience or two and someone wasn't taking any chances that I might've been hired to come after them.'

Link Waterman drew himself up to his full height, face cold and sober. 'Either way, you quit my town right after breakfast!'

Durango smiled faintly and nodded: let him have that one, too. He was mighty tired of Waterman and his touchy ego.

'Long as I can get fixed-up with another room so's I can get a good night's sleep.'

'Hey, honey!' the woman said suddenly, recovering fast now. 'Ask for one with a double bed. I'm all paid for and, like you said, I owe you somethin' for savin' my life!'

4

THE VALLEY

Durango was in no hurry to leave town and ate a leisurely breakfast in the hotel dining-room, then settled his bill, gathered his gear and picked up his horse at the livery.

He smiled half to himself as he saw Sheriff Waterman sitting on the rail of the porch outside his office, smoking, looking mighty serious as he watched the gunfighter ride slowly by. *Great on looking tough, not so great acting that way . . .*

‘’Mornin’, Sheriff. Looks like a nice day.’

‘Now that you’re leavin’ it’ll be nice.’

Durango laughed quietly, touched a hand to his hat brim and rode on. He was not surprised when he heard the lawman’s voice behind him call, ‘Don’t bother comin' back!'

He rode out of town over the bridge he had used when he had first arrived, watching every alley between buildings on the approaches, and then the bushes and scattered trees as his mount clopped across the wooden arch. All seemed clear this morning. No ambushes. Not likely to be, either, after three men had failed. Which wasn't to say that later on, if he was still around, someone wouldn't try again. He hadn't known any of the men who had tried to kill him: they had obviously been hired just for that job. All seemed to have lived on the fringe of the law, hiring out for anything that would pay a few dollars: not too fussy about why.

Someone was scared of him, that was for sure. But . . . three men: they hadn't necessarily been hired by the same man. Two were in the alley, ready to backshoot him. The other — well, it was a mite different. Bribing the whore to lie naked on his bed and distract him was a little more refined — maybe by someone who had done this kind of thing before. Carey, they said his name was: or it was just the one he was using around here. The one they would carve on his headboard in Boot Hill, that was for sure.

By now he was into the foothills, making for the pass that led to Killdeer Valley and he rode with his rifle across his thighs, eyes restlessly roving the slopes and the shadows and any rocks large enough to hide a crouching man with a gun.

No one tried to shoot him before he reached the pass. The sides were high, the trail narrow. Good place for an ambush. He paused on a low knoll right at the entrance to light a cigarillo. After he had smoked some of it he was satisfied the pass was safe to travel through, but he rode carefully, walking the horse to start, suddenly spurring it to a run, angling in on a clump of rocks. Then another fast dash to the next cover — and beyond lay Killdeer Valley.

He paused long enough to finish the cigarillo, rode to the next knoll and dismounted by some bushes. Using them for cover, he brought out a crumpled piece of paper that contained a crudely drawn map and written directions. From these he found the part of the valley he was interested in, swept his field-glasses around, slowing and changing the focus as he saw two large ranch houses, one on the rising slopes, the other on the flats near a bend in one of the rivers which meandered through this area. The glasses weren't good enough to allow him to pick out the brands, but the grazing cattle looked healthy. And there were plenty.

Then he swept the glasses on slowly, past the ranches and their obvious pastures, trying to focus on some smaller holdings at the far end of the valley, flat bottomland mostly. It was too far away for him to get much detail, so he put the glasses back in their leather case and slung it from the saddle before mounting. Giving the immediate area of the two big spreads a wide berth, he rode towards the distant end of Killdeer Valley.

* * *

Big John Dancey was sitting at his ease in the shade of the cottonwood at one end of Brant Collier's large ranch house. Here on the rise, they could see a long way up the valley and he had spotted a cone of dust, likely from a lone rider, drifting across the north-west end before it dissipated over the slight rise.

Collier tapped his fingers on the edge of the round table that held the drinks, watching Dancey swing his gaze back to his face.

'I'm right, aren't I, Brant?' Dancey said quietly. 'I know you've used Carey before on a couple of off-colour deals. You even let slip once you had somethin' on him, but didn't go into details.'

'That's your story,' Collier growled. 'Sure, I've used Carey a coupla times. He's a good horseman and knows cattle. One of the best brush-poppers I've seen. An' he works cheap.'

Dancey smiled thinly. 'Not any more. Hear he paid that whore a hundred bucks to spread herself on Durango's bed, kind of catch his eye, you know what I mean?'

'Man's got more money than sense then. Wouldn't catch me payin' no whore a hundred bucks. Hell, even in Cheyenne at the Prime Cut, a hundred'd buy you more gals than you could handle in a week.'

'Maybe more'n *you* could handle.' Dancey turned his glass slowly between his fingers. 'And maybe it weren't Carey's money, anyway.'

Collier frowned and took his time about meeting the other's gaze. 'Get to it, John! You gonna come right out and accuse me of sendin' Carey to jump that gunfighter, whyn't you damn well say so?'

'Consider it said.' Dancey leaned forward in his chair. 'Brant, I've always wondered about you. You never use banks, yet when you need money, you come up with it somehow and always in cash.'

'Where I keep my money is my business!' Collier was curt, his mouth tight, eyes angry.

Dancey held up a hand briefly. 'Fair enough. I ain't after any of your money, if that's what you think. But I've had a notion you keep it close by. And I've wondered if you don't use banks 'cause your money is traceable.'

Collier's hand shook as he poured fresh whiskey into both glasses. He avoided looking at Dancey directly. 'Traceable to what?' he asked huskily.

Dancey shrugged. 'Aw, I dunno — maybe some past robbery, express box, payroll, somethin' like that.'

'Watch where you're goin' with this, John!'

'I know where I'm goin' with it. Brant, I figure you hired Carey to kill

Durango; maybe used what you know about him to get him to do it, because while Carey's beat-up some nesters pretty badly so one of 'em died, I never heard of him killin' anyone in cold blood. But, he's got a price like everyone else, I guess, and if you wanted Durango dead bad enough, you might've paid it.'

Collier remained silent, staring into his glass now. After a long, drawn-out moment, he said, 'Well, seems to me, the main thing is Durango's still walkin' around. Three men tried to nail him and he killed them all.'

'Says somethin' about him, don't it?'

Collier made an impatient gesture. 'Hell, everyone knows he's mighty fast with a gun — likely why them idiots tried to bushwhack him.'

''Course it is. Other reason is they were paid to do it. Sure weren't their own idea, not Tooth and Tom Nye.'

Brant Collier lifted his deadpan face slowly and looked steadily at Dancey. 'Mebbe they were hired but not . . . by . . . me.'

'I believe that, Brant, 'bout them two, leastways.'

Collier said nothing. Then Dancey tossed down his drink and stood up, reaching for his hat resting on a vacant chair. 'Well, I'll be gettin' back to the spread. By the by, I had a word with Case. He won't admit to nothin', but I figure mebbe he hired Perry Tooth and Tom Nye to backshoot Durango. They've worked for him before; like beat-up a couple sodbusters, tore down fences, when Nebraska wasn't available.'

'Be his style, I reckon. Always close-mouthed about his past.'

'Ain't we all? OK, Brant. I still think whoever sent for Durango wants him to buy into this problem we got with the nesters and the free range. Nothin' else.'

'I hear Waterman hates the sound of Durango's name: might be a chance to get ol' Link on our side.'

Dancey looked receptive to that, arching his eyebrows, pursing his lips, nodding slowly. 'Just might be what we need, somethin' to get him down off that damn fence he's been straddlin' for — *What the hell's he doin' here?*'

Collier gazed the way Dancey was facing and saw a rider coming in fast, sliding his mount down the slope and raising enough dust to choke a buffalo. Then he saw the piebald through the roiling clouds and knew it was Arlo Jeffries.

They waited till Dancey's foreman skidded his mount to a halt near Collier's corrals, hit the dirt running, stopping at the foot of the porch steps. He leaned on the short rail, searching for enough breath to speak. His eyes went to Dancey. 'Durango — '

'You're s'posed to be watchin' him,' Dancey growled and Arlo nodded several times.

'Did. He rid nor'-west, up valley.'

'The hell you say!'

'Yep, an' you won't believe where he stopped.'

'I won't know that till you tell me, damnit!'

Arlo grinned. 'One of the sod-busters musta sent for him.'

'*Which* one, goddammit?' grated Dancey. Collier's hands were white where they gripped the rail he was now leaning on.

Savouring the moment, Arlo Jeffries looked from one rancher to the other. 'Could hardly believe it myself, but — OK, OK, boss! It was Della Shaw! He rode into her yard an' she come a'runnin' outa her house and threw her arms around his neck like a long-lost lover!'

'Della!' Dancey was incredulous.

'Where the hell would she get enough money to hire a man like Durango?' demanded Collier, his voice kind of shaky. 'Even if the other homesteaders chipped in — '

'You don't listen good, Brant!' Dancey said sourly. 'Arlo just said she ran to him, threw her arms around him! A good-lookin' gal like Della who does that to a man don't need money, for Chris'sakes!'

* * *

Dancey was wrong.

Della Shaw didn't run up to Durango when she recognized him and throw welcoming arms about him.

She was holding a half-moon leather knife she had been using at the outdoor bench to cut a saddle-bag flap from a newly tanned hide. As soon as she recognized Durango dismounting, she leapt to her feet and ran at him, knife in hand, swiping at his neck, blade aimed at the jugular.

He caught the wrist and twisted, making her half-turn her body to ease the sudden pain. She stumbled close in against his lean hard length.

From a distance, it must have looked like she was welcoming him with her whole being. Her other arm flailed around his neck as the fingers clawed up towards his eyes.

By the time Durango got his chin tucked in and wrenched his head to one side, it looked as if he was getting his face in position to kiss her.

By that time, Arlo Jeffries had run back to his piebald and hit the stirrup, spurring the animal the moment he dropped into the saddle: he figured Dancey would be pleased to know this.

Durango had both her wrists held behind her back by now, the leather knife trampled underfoot. Her face was flushed, white teeth gritted, dark eyes flashing. Wavy brown hair spilled half across her face. She shook her head angrily to clear it, pursed her lips to spit in his face.

He wrenched her arms painfully and she gulped, cried out, sagging a little. He supported her, spun her around and anchored her against him with his powerful arms.

'For God's sake, Della! Calm down!'

She didn't say anything coherent, struggled violently, trying to kick him, but he spread his feet and she missed.

She twisted and turned as much as she could, snapped her head back, trying to break his nose. He got his head aside just in time but still felt the blow of her skull against a cheekbone. He shook her roughly.

'*Goddammit, woman! Be still!*'

Her teeth clacked together and her ribs hurt, her head snapping painfully on her neck. Despite herself she sagged, legs feeling weak. Her diaphragm convulsed with a sob and then she was cussing him out — using some pretty raw bunkhouse expletives, too — but she was running down, the first flare of anger having been frustrated by his speedy resistance to her attack.

He let her sob and then heard her swearing at herself in a low, gasping voice. He looked around but there were no ranch hands in sight who might try a Galahad act on behalf of their boss, and attempt to 'rescue' her.

'Della — I came about Beau.'

She twisted her tear-stained face towards him as far as she could see over her shoulder. 'You got him killed! You sent him out of that . . . that damn cabin *first!* Let those outlaws shoot him . . . to . . . to ribbons! You yellow *bastard!*'

Again, she tried to get at him but he held her easily enough now, moved in against the clapboard wall of the small barn and crushed her against it, pinning her.

'You're hurting me — damn you!'

'And it could get worse unless you stand still long enough to listen — will you?'

'I have no interest in anything you have to say! I-I just want to kill you!'

'That's because you been listening to rumours and trail talk. I never sent Beau outa that cabin into a hail of gunfire. He went of his own accord.'

'Of course you would say that!'

'S'pose I would. But they had us trapped and I'd been hit pretty bad, so I gave Beau the last of my ammunition, and he tried to make a break for it and bring help.'

He felt her stiffen a little and caught a side view of her face as she frowned uncertainly. 'That . . . that sounds like Beau,' she whispered. '*He* was brave!'

'Yeah. I was bleeding like a stuck hog from a hole in my side: I'll show you the scar if you want. It's not long healed. Anyway, Beau didn't make it, of course. There were four of them and we thought there was only two. He staggered back inside and collapsed across my legs, pushing the sixguns into my lap.' He paused, remembering the young Shaw, blood on his mouth, his body pocked with bleeding holes, hands shaking and eyes pleading. 'Each gun had three shells in it and then the outlaws rushed the cabin. I got three, wounded the fourth, man named Sundeen, but he got away . . . '

He paused again, remembering the wounded killer who called himself Sundeen. It had taken a long time for the wound in his side to heal. Longer still to finally track down Sundeen in a hidey-hole back of Deadwood. The man had had a half-breed pard with him, heard Durango was coming for him, and tried to murder him in a night camp in the Black Hills by a swift-flowing creek. They had shot up the bedroll he had packed with old clothes to look like someone sleeping there. Then he had come drifting in on a log where he had waited for their arrival. Two shots apiece, and it was finished — Beau Shaw was avenged.

But could he get this woman, Beau's sister, to believe that?

He had ridden far to bring her Beau's belongings and the news that her brother had been avenged — he savvied her reaction to his arrival, but he *would* make her believe him. *He had to, or she'd damn well kill him!*

'Let's go inside and talk over a cup of java,' he suggested, pushing her towards the log cabin ranch house he knew Beau had built. 'Beau always said you make great coffee.'

'I'd like to make yours with rat poison!' she hissed, staggering as he shoved her roughly.

Suddenly he grinned. She was a spitfire, all right. Beau had warned him, for they had been on their way here when they had run foul of Sundeen and his men.

Uneasily, he followed her into the cabin's small kitchen. *By God, he'd watch every damn move she made! She hadn't sounded like she was joshing when she said she'd feed him rat poison . . . And she wasn't yet convinced he wasn't responsible for Beau's death.*

She could turn out to be more of a danger to him than those three bushwhackers.

5

HERO

Durango watched her every movement as she made the coffee and was satisfied that she had not slipped anything extra in with the grounds. But, as she set it heating on the wood-fired stove, he should have been watching her other hand, the one screened by her body.

As he drew out a chair to sit at the table, she lunged at him and he glimpsed light flashing from a long sharp blade. He was still bent forward as he eased out the chair, suddenly rolled across the table, flailing his legs. The knife blade thudded into the deal top, burying itself two inches in the wood. Sobbing with effort, she tugged wildly to free the knife. By then Durango had swung up one leg, placed his boot against her chest and straightened the leg abruptly.

She cried out as she was hurled across the kitchen, the knife still quivering in the table. She crashed into a closed pantry door and he heard things inside falling from the shelves as her legs folded and she dropped to her knees, gasping. He snapped the point off the knife and threw it to one side, grabbed her under the arms and dumped her on a straight-back chair. She had had the wind taken out of her and she sagged forward, fighting for breath.

By then he had found her supply of empty floursacks in the pantry — most pioneer women kept the calico sacks and put them to good use in many ways, from cleaning rags to clothes, dyeing the calico to their liking. Durango hastily tore one into wide strips and bound the girl's arms to the back of the chair. By then she had regained most of her breath and while she shouted her protests there was real worry in her face now as he made for the door.

'Where — where are you going?' she called but he didn't answer.

Shortly he returned to the kitchen and placed his saddle-bags on the table. The coffee was ready and he poured two cups. He added a little cold water to hers from the sink pump and held it to her lips. Her big brown eyes looked up warily yet defiantly.

'I don't think there's any rat poison in this, but you drink first anyway.'

She smiled crookedly. 'Got you worried, have I?'

He pushed the mug against her teeth and she took a swallow, her eyes mocking now. 'See? No effect. It's safe for you to drink, Mr Scaredy Cat!'

He almost smiled at the schoolyard taunt, sipped some of his own coffee, sitting down opposite her. 'Mmm — not bad.' He dragged the saddle-bags across, unbuckled the straps and upended them. Several items spilled out, including a battered sixgun that had seen a lot of use.

'That's Beau's! It was Dad's originally.'

Durango nodded. 'He told me. Said it was the only thing you had left of your father's, except for his old tin watch which was busted. I thought you might like to have it, seeing as Beau was the last one to use it. Except for me.'

Her eyes were moist now. 'You don't count,' she said softly in a voice that quavered. 'Is this the gun he had when you pushed him outside the cabin?'

His own eyes were chips of granite. 'No, it's the gun he took along with him, when *he* decided to make a break, to try and lead them away from me. I passed out from loss of blood. I guess he figured they'd think I was dead, go after him, but he'd have a head start by that time and hoped to reach help. I was too damn weak to try to stop him.'

He expected her to scoff as she had previously, but she kept looking at him, quietly sobbing now. He pointed.

'Beau's jack-knife. His neckerchief

— he was kinda partial to that, washed it every day, smoothed it out so it'd look good when he tied it round his neck . . . you gave it to him, I believe.'

She nodded, lips tight, tears running down her cheeks. 'For his eighteenth birthday.' She watched him lift Beau's trouser belt with the silver buckle that he had won in a buck-jumping contest in Cheyenne. Lastly he put the pair of scratched, bent brass spurs with one rowel shank snapped, on the table. *She remembered Beau breaking that spur . . . she remembered so much now . . .*

'It ain't much. There was no money except a half-dollar. I put another one to it, placed 'em on his eyes when I buried him.'

Her lips parted and she frowned, no longer struggling against her bonds. 'Why did you do that?'

He shrugged and didn't answer but she kept at him and he told her quietly, 'Old Indian superstition. A man takes money to offer the Great Spirit to ensure his soul doesn't wander forever between the winds, then it'll find a resting place somewhere in the Happy Hunting Grounds.'

He heard her breath hiss in through her nostrils. 'That's what Moon Warrior used to tell us when we were kids!'

'Yeah, Beau told me. Some crippled old Lakota your father kept around for no good reason, except he had a soft streak for lame ducks.'

Her face suddenly softened. 'You understand that? So many people could never see why Dad kept Moon around, never used him, just enjoyed his company. I-I have to thank you for taking the trouble to do that — for Beau — I know he believed in that kind of thing.'

He smiled and held up a hand. 'Yeah. He was mighty young — in outlook as well as years. I know how hard it was for you to say that, so whatever else was to follow — consider it said. I didn't mind doing it. Maybe someone'll do it when they bury me.' *He hadn't meant to say that!*

Her brimming eyes were wandering towards the things spread out on the table, lifting again to his sober face, obviously perplexed by this warmer side of him. 'What did happen up at that cabin?'

'Sundeen jumped us — we — I was kind of careless, fell for one of his tricks and we came to the cabin and he was waiting with his pards and opened up. Traded a lot of lead before I was hit by a ricochet. Bled like hell. Beau kept saying I had to have a sawbones. Then when he saw how low on ammo we were he made a dash for it to try for help . . . I told you before.'

'And they killed him. But first he crawled back to give you his gun with what was left of the bullets . . . '

He nodded.

'It must've been difficult for you to bury Beau with a wound like that.'

'Didn't matter. I was obligated.'

She slumped against the floursack strips, crying openly now. 'And you took the trouble to bring me his things and I-I tried to kill you . . . '

'I'm just glad you stuck to knives, 'cause Beau said you're a damn good shot, too.'

She laughed halfway through a sob and nearly choked and by the time she had settled, he had freed her and sat back, sipping his coffee while she rubbed her arms briskly.

'I-I'm sorry, Durango.'

'As long as we've sorted it out now.'

'Yes, I think we have. You'll stay for a meal, of course . . . ?'

He hesitated briefly, then nodded. 'Sure. Thanks.'

* * *

It was a good meal, simple food but cooked well. They ate mostly in silence and afterwards she went behind a strung blanket and came out with a pile of tattered papers in a cardboard folder.

'This place isn't big enough for two bedrooms. Beau strung the blanket across the corner and slept in there.'

She set down the folder, flipped the cardboard — and Durango looked down at a wanted dodger with his picture on it.

But the name beneath wasn't Durango.

'Clete Williams is your real name, I take it?' she said and he nodded, picking up the dodger.

'After that fracas with the Claytons, they started calling me Durango so I dropped the Clete Williams — This dodger's pretty damn old. Put out by the father of a crazy kid who forced me into a gunfight down in El Paso. I went on the run and a lot of men tried to collect the reward. That's when I put in a mighty lot of practice on my draw.'

'That was where your reputation as a fast gun began?' He looked up quickly and she smiled. 'Beau told me. He was impressed when you faced those four killers in Durango and out-drew them all. That's when he started following your exploits, went out of his way to find newspaper articles and any news at all about you. He was only sixteen, and we lived an isolated life. He was looking for a hero, someone to take Dad's place, I think. He was so anxious to meet you!'

He looked uncomfortable. 'Never had anyone look on me as a kinda hero before.'

'Beau did. I couldn't make him see that you were just a killer, no matter how glamorized by the papers.' There was defiance in her words and look.

'Sure. Don't blame you. He was just a kid. Bothered me no end when he rode into my camp one day and said he was gonna be my sidekick.' He shook his head, remembering how he had tried and threatened and cussed in an effort to shake the obsessed kid. All to no avail.

Then there was that time in Laramie. He thought he'd lost Beau long ago, when two brothers named Danton who had been trailing him for a hundred miles because he'd downed their father in a gunfight, burst into his camp and tied him to a tree after beating him.

They were lining up to take turns at shooting him to pieces when Beau Shaw came crashing out of the brush, his father's old sixgun thundering in his hand as he fanned the hammer. The Dantons never knew what hit them, both doing a crazy dance as the lead thudded into them, knocked them against each other as they fell in a heap. They were both dead before they hit the ground.

The kid looked kind of wild-eyed, flushed with the thrill and excitement of what he had done. He could hardly speak when he grinned widely at the battered Durango.

'Read how you did that in Santa Fe. Mr Ned Buntline described it in detail.'

'Mr Buntline got it all wrong,' gasped Durango, head hanging, the ropes biting into his chest and arms. 'Fanning a gun is . . . loco . . . bullets fly all over the place. You've gotta be . . . close.'

A mite more sober, the kid said, gesturing to the dead men, 'Sometimes they fly straight!'

Despite his pain, Durango had smiled. 'Yeah, sometimes when you're close like you were, and you're lucky.'

As the kid cut him loose and helped him to his bedroll, Beau said, 'See? You do need a sidekick.'

Coming back to Della Shaw's kitchen Durango told her about the incident and added, 'I could hardly turn him down after he'd just saved my neck.'

Her eyes were narrowed. 'I hated you more than ever when Beau wrote me and told me he was at last riding with you . . . I knew you'd get him killed.'

He lit a cigarillo, avoiding her gaze. Then he looked at her through the first cloud of smoke. 'So did I. But he was good. A good learner and a good shot. Never very fast, but — well, he didn't hunt trouble and we rode a lot of miles together. We had some fun.'

'Fun! My God! Killing people is fun?'

'Beau wasn't a killer. I never hunted trouble. I kept him away from towns and places I figured might be dangerous. I reckoned on dumping him after a while. You know, let him side me for a few weeks as a kind of . . . reward.'

'For saving your life! His *reward* was to ride with you and risk his own life in more gunfights!'

'Told you, I tried to make sure we didn't ride into any real trouble.'

'A man like you! How could you ever hope to avoid trouble with your reputation?'

He studied the burning end of his cigarillo silently for a time, then raised his eyes to her. 'Yeah. Beau was a likeable kid, damn good company. I guess I just put off the time when I aimed to dump him . . . left it too late.'

Her face was sober. *She saw how this actually bothered him!* 'Beau would've found you again.' She spoke quietly but there was a catch in her voice and he saw her small hands were closed tightly in her lap.

'Yeah, I knew that, too. But I had to try. I didn't want him getting hurt . . . '

'And finally you led him into a situation that got him killed!'

He nodded. He saw she was waiting for him to say something, but he didn't speak. *Hell, he'd said it all a hundred times to himself, over and over. Why the hell hadn't he shaken the kid before? Did he actually* enjoy *the hero-worship?*

There was a sour taste in his mouth even thinking that.

Suddenly, she stood up. 'Well, I thank you for returning Beau's things. I-I guess it was difficult. Beau was such an intense kind of boy.'

'I ought to've been tougher with him. But it was mighty hard. An eager youngster, always smiling, practised by the hour with his gun, hung on my every word. I'm damn sorry he got killed. If he hadn't — I wouldn't be here.'

'No.' It was flat and a lot could be read into that single word.

'Thanks for the meal. I hope you savvy how things were.'

She hesitated, then nodded briefly. 'It's not easy. But, I do. I believe you are truly contrite, Durango. If I didn't, I might — well, we won't go into that.' She tossed her head again. 'You have people worried around these parts, you know.'

He smiled faintly as he nodded. 'That's their problem.'

'It's rather amusing. It's a stuck-up town in many ways, and to see some of the pillars of the community so worried because they think you might have been hired to kill them for some past misdemeanour — well, it brings them down the scale a few notches.'

He chuckled. 'Yeah. Specially as there's some trouble over range rights or something in this valley. I picked up that much in gossip.'

She was sober again now. 'Yes. Three of the big ranchers, Dancey, Collier and Case, had this valley to themselves for years. Now that the government has approved part of it for homesteading, they feel threatened, say they'll lose range they've been able to use for grazing for many years and, of course, our fences don't please them.'

'You — yourself, I mean — you're having trouble with these big spreads?'

'No more than any of the other homesteaders.'

He frowned. 'This is a long way up the valley from the big ranches I saw.'

She laughed shortly, bitterly. 'Those three regard the entire Killdeer Valley as theirs. Every foot, every bush, every drop of water. Oh, they have plenty of range and more than adequate graze, but they've gotten used to a certain way of living over the years, used to folk jumping when they say jump and showing them deference if not respect. Now they see all of that endangered.'

'I didn't see any hands working this place when I rode in,' he said quietly, with a steady gaze.

She gave him a sharp glance. 'No. My last man was beaten up last week. It took him three days to recover and then he packed his warbag, and no one's seen him since . . . I can't blame him. Josh Morcom's rider was beaten so badly he died. They claimed he was in a drunken brawl.'

'I've seen this kind of thing before. Someone hires a gunfighter like me to back them. The other side hires *two* gunfighters, and pretty damn soon you have a full-scale range war . . . ' He paused and then nodded to himself. 'That's what's got Link Waterman so edgy, huh? Afraid I'm about to start a range war.'

'Yes, I suppose that's how he sees it — how most of the valley sees it. When I heard you had come here, the first thing I thought of was that one of the big three had brought you in to drive us out once and for all.'

'And the second thing you thought of?' He asked with a wry smile, and she flushed a little but tossed her head.

'I thought at last I was going to get a chance to kill you for what you'd done to Beau.' She had the grace to flush and avoid his gaze. 'Or, what I believed you'd done.'

He nodded, smiling faintly. 'That's

what I figured.' He picked up his saddle-bag. 'Well, if you've got that out of your system, I'd best be on my way.'

Then they heard the clatter of hoofs in the yard, the creak of harness as horses were hauled to a stop — a lot of horses.

Someone called, 'Hey, gunfighter! We want a word with you! Step outside, an' keep your hands where we can see 'em! No one'll get hurt if you're reasonable. If you're not: well, the odds are agin even you, Durango!'

6

CHAMPION

Peering through the curtains, the girl at his side, one hand on his gun butt, Durango counted nine riders gathered in a half-circle around the front of the cabin. There was a big man sitting a roan horse a few paces in front of the others.

Apparently, he was the one who had called out.

Durango felt the girl stiffen beside him. 'That's Big John Dancey! And there are men there from Case and Collier, too!' She turned to him. 'The Big Three Alliance!'

'C'mon, gunfighter!' Dancey called again, a mocking tone to his words. 'Don't tell me the Durango Gunhawk is scared to square-off to just ten men!'

The riders chuckled and he saw the

sun flashing from unsheathed rifles and sixguns.

The girl sucked down a sharp breath and placed a hand on his arm which he shook off immediately, startling her. Then she saw it was his gun arm she had touched.

'Sorry. What're you going to do?'

'Go see what they want.'

'But — '

'Stay here. Lock the other door. Don't come out.'

'But you can't go out there!'

'Stay put! This is my kind of deal.'

Then he was striding to the front door, yanked it open and stepped out into the sunlight just past the stoop.

'You can't count, Dancey, I make it only nine of you.'

Big John Dancey grinned. 'No — there's ten.'

His gaze slid past Durango's shoulder even as the gunfighter whirled — but paused, gun almost clear of leather.

Della Shaw was in the doorway, held

in the grip of Arlo Jeffries, a pistol pressed against her head, a hand covering her mouth. *Must've come in the back door while Durango's attention was on the front!*

Durango let his gun fall back into the holster and stepped to one side where he could watch the mounted men and Arlo and the girl all at the same time. Dancey seemed at his ease, hands folded now on the saddle-horn, very confident.

'Now we know who hired you, gunfighter.' The big rancher glared at the struggling girl. 'But won't do you no good. You're leavin' this valley. Just how is up to you.'

'I've got a choice?' asked Durango, eyes restless: he didn't sound all that interested in Dancey's reply.

Riding high, Dancey smiled crookedly. 'Sure — we're fair. You can ride out now and we all part friends, or you can go out draped over a horse, headed straight for an open grave on Boot Hill.'

Durango shook his head. 'Don't

fancy your Boot Hill as my last resting place, Dancey.'

The rancher spread his hands. 'Me neither. So, you can just ride on out — er — escorted by me and my men, of course.'

'Sure, that's how it'd be . . . if I was leaving.'

Even though Arlo Jeffries' hand was covering the girl's mouth, Durango heard the hiss of her indrawn breath. Glancing at her briefly, he saw her eyes imploring him not to try to stand up to these men. He returned his gaze to Dancey who was sober now, with maybe a slight hint of worry. But he covered it with a brief laugh.

'We all know your rep with a gun, but you goin' up agin ten men? Your lady friend also under a gun . . . ? Nah — can't see that happenin'.'

'Stand by,' Durango told him quietly. Before the words had even reached Dancey there was an explosion and Jeffries cried out as one of his legs, showing between the girl's, jerked out violently from under him. He fell awkwardly, dragging Della halfway down. In an instant she kicked him in the chest and dived back through the doorway. By then, Durango was covering the stunned riders.

'God almighty!' someone breathed. 'D'ya see that?'

'I seen nothin' — only Arlo going down! Never even seen Durango draw!'

There was more murmuring but it faded fast as Durango addressed the silent Dancey who now sat stiffly. 'You go next, Dancey. I've got five shots and five of you are gonna die if you don't do like I say.' He swept the gun barrel in a short arc. 'Any volunteers?'

They were all tense and wide-eyed now. Dancey had to clear his throat. 'You'll die, too.'

'Won't do you any good — or the other four I take with me.'

The riders had seen enough, remembered back in town there were three fresh graves on Boot Hill. A couple slid their guns back into holsters and most of the others followed, one by one. Jeffries moaned and writhed, holding his bleeding leg, trying to wrench off his neckerchief with one hand.

Then the girl appeared from inside the cabin with a double-barrelled shotgun, both hammers cocked. 'Whoever Durango leaves alive, can have the fun of dodging a double charge of buckshot,' she said tautly.

Dancey sat like a centaur: frozen, nonplussed, unable to cope with the situation that had turned his original plans upside down so suddenly. Now he was the one having to decide whether to ride out or die.

'You got anything to say?' Durango asked Dancey.

'We don't want a range war.' Dancey knew it was limp, but he couldn't think of anything else. Never in his life had his brain been numbed so fully as right now. One moment Durango was talking, next Arlo was screaming in pain down in the dust, and the girl lunged back into the cabin. His head whirled and his stomach knotted painfully.

'I'll bet you don't: a range war usually attracts the attention of US marshals. You just aimed to bully the homesteaders and ride roughshod over 'em, huh? I guess you'd only call it a range war if they started to fight back.'

'And we have started!' Della said flatly, but Dancey didn't look at her. He was watching Durango mighty warily.

'My family opened up this valley. Case and Brant Collier came along later and we shared, them bein' cowmen. We been here for years, runnin' our cattle, puttin' money into the town. Hell, I'm even lobbyin' to get us a railhead.' There was a slight hurt back there in his words. 'Then the damn gov'ment throws open the valley for homesteadin', an' we gotta pull back from land we been usin' for years and have our cows and mounts tore up on bob-wire fences! Hell, you call that fair?'

'I savvy how you and your pards must feel, Dancey.'

Dancey was regaining some of his confidence now and managed a sneer. 'Sure — and if we'd hired you, you'd be kickin' the asses of these sodbusters! You can be bought, Durango!'

He said this last breathlessly with a rush and kind of flinched when the gunfighter's steely eyes settled on his face. 'My gun can be bought, Dancey, I'm my own man.'

'Ah, hell! You ain't tellin' me you got a conscience!' Dancey glanced around at his own men, but they were still worrying about where they were going to be if the bullets started to fly — and most of them were thinking if Dancey didn't shut up and quit riling this Durango gunhawk, they were going to find out in a damn hurry!

'I ride for the brand, Dancey, but I ride my own trail.'

'Means you'll quit if you feel like it?'

'Means what I said. Now, you take your men, including that cry-baby lying on the ground: he's not bad hit. If I'd wanted to bust his leg I would've: it's just a flesh wound. But you ride back to your spread and tell your pards to leave this end of the valley alone. Hell, you got about nine-tenths of it still. Put away your pride and your greed and everyone can get on with their lives and make a quiet living.'

'You don't really savvy what you're up against. She ain't told you the full story. You'll surely earn every dollar she and them other sodbusters are payin' you, I'm tellin' you true, mister. An' mebbe you won't get a chance to spend 'em!'

'I've seen greedy, bullying land-grabbers like you before, just aiming to show everyone they're the big frog in the pond. You heed what I say, Dancey. Think it over.'

The rancher had found his old confidence again now that he felt Durango wasn't going to cut him down in cold blood. He shook his head slowly.

'Mister, you're the one oughta listen! Think I'll have Case and Collier chip in and we'll buy you a nice marble headstone with your name carved in gold — '

'Tell the stonemason to leave the name-plate blank,' Durango said. 'With enough room for three names.'

Dancey's smile faded a little but he forced it back. 'Pete, Max, get Arlo on his horse.'

'Wait,' said Della. 'I'll bandage his leg first.'

* * *

Durango reloaded his pistol as the dustcloud swirled across Della's front yard, squinting to watch that none of the riders broke away from the main group. But they weren't that stupid. They all headed back up-valley.

'I-I've never seen anything like that before,' the girl said. 'One man facing down *ten*! And they're hardcases.'

'Seemed like time to make a stand.'

'Are you really going to stay? I mean, we need someone like you, but I don't think any of the homesteaders can find enough money to pay you. Maybe if we pooled our funds we could manage.'

'Just keep cooking those elegant meals.' He grinned. 'When I start getting indigestion, I'll ride on.'

She couldn't believe her ears, but suddenly smiled, then sobered almost immediately, facing him squarely. 'You're the last man I ever thought would be helping me and my friends. Why're you doing this? Is it because of Beau?'

'Partly. I liked that kid and I owe him my life.' He glanced off towards the fading dustcloud. 'And I don't like bullies who figure they can stride around in seven-league boots, stomping everyone who gets in their way.'

'We-we surely need a man like you on our side, Durango.'

He nodded. 'Dancey mentioned someone named Case — Jason Case by any chance?'

She snapped up her head. 'Yes. That's his name. They call him Jace, sometimes J.C. D'you know him?'

'Could be. You might've heard of the trouble in the Black Hills a while back, between miners and cattlemen?'

'Oh, yes, I remember. It turned into a dreadful range war — there was lots of killing . . . ' Her voice trailed off. 'You were there?'

He nodded. 'Just at the last. While some miners were trading lead with a bunch of cattlemen, someone got into the assay office, stole a big haul of nuggets and grain gold. Never recovered, but I recall that one of the cowmen named Jason Case quit soon after and the word was he'd stolen the gold . . . him and his sidekick, a long streak of misery calling himself Nebraska.'

He heard the quick indrawn breath again. 'That — he's Case's foreman! A very mean type, always picking fights. He's massive, and uses his size to intimidate.'

'That's Nebraska. He shot me in the back once, left me for dead.'

Della frowned. 'I see — is this going

to be a private vendetta now?'

'It'll be whatever comes of it, Della. Don't think you're getting any bargain in me. I'll attract more trouble than a dead cat does flies — specially if those cowmen put a bounty on my head. Which they could do: it's happened before.'

Her concern showed clearly. 'Perhaps it's not such a good idea you buying into this feud, Durango. I mean, you live a precarious life as it is, never knowing when someone is going to force you into a shoot-out and — ' She stopped.

He smiled slightly. 'Go ahead, say it — and one time I'll go up against someone faster. Has to happen. Nothing I can do about it. I don't worry about such things any longer. I reckon it's about time I chose which side I fight on, instead of letting the number of dollars decide for me.'

'There probably won't be *any* dollars.'

He held up a hand quickly. 'Just leave

it at that, Della.'

Her smile warmed and brightened her face. 'I don't know why I ever thought you were nothing more than just a cold-blooded killer.'

'That's just my good side — wait'll you see my other one.'

7

OLD ENEMIES

Durango rode slowly towards the arched wooden bridge across the narrowest part of the river at the north end of town.

Inwardly, he smiled wryly, knowing Link Waterman's reaction would be one of hostility at his appearance so soon after leaving Two Rivers. He had asked Della Shaw about men to work her quarter-section and immediately she had looked worried.

'Well, I don't really know. I've had a couple of men from town or who were riding through the valley actually looking for work but Dancey and his friends soon sought them out and . . . 'persuaded' them that it would be healthier for them to work elsewhere.'

'They just quit, or keep riding?'

'The first two men didn't. They said they'd work where they wanted to. But the very next time they went to town there was some sort of argument with a few of Dancey's men and — '

'Waterman made no move against Dancey's men?'

'Durango, it was all arranged with plenty of witnesses to say my men started the whole thing — Link Waterman could easily have found out the truth but essentially he's a lazy man and as long as appearances seem logical enough he'll settle for that. He's good for this town, but at a price.'

Durango nodded. 'Know the kind of sheriff you mean. Reckon I'd find someone to come work for you if I went in looking?'

She seemed wary when she answered. 'You might — word would have gotten around by now how you shot Arlo Jeffries and maybe someone has spoken about the way you buffaloed Big John Dancey and nine of his men.' She suddenly brightened. 'Yes! I think you just might find someone who's willing to work in the valley, with you on the same side, but you have to remember you aren't in the sheriff's good books.'

'Reckon that won't make me lose any sleep . . . '

And here he was now riding slowly down Main, seeing some people stop to stare, others pretending not to notice him. Link Waterman's office door opened and he stomped out onto his landing, leaning on the rail and calling, 'I told you not to come back, gunfighter!'

'Got me a job out in the valley, Sheriff. Foreman for Della Shaw. Just in to pick up a few supplies and see if anyone wants to work for the BDS.'

Waterman straightened, eyes narrowed. 'I heard it was Della hired you — couldn't believe it. You give her a cut rate?'

Durango slowed and leaned on the saddlehorn, smiling easily. 'She didn't hire my gun, Sheriff, if that's what you're thinking. No one hired me to come here — like I've been trying to convince some folk ever since I arrived. I had private business with Della and, as she's short-handed, I'm staying to help out.' His face straightened and his voice hardened. 'Now you wouldn't grudge a struggling homesteader like Della a top hand, would you?'

Folk were gathering now to hear this, exchanging glances, some beginning to smile when they recalled how some of the town's 'upstanding' citizens had reacted to Durango's arrival.

The words *Guilty consciences* were bandied about freely.

Then Waterman answered. 'Mebbe I don't believe you didn't come here with your gun already paid for.'

'Makes no nevermind to me what you believe, Sheriff. I'm working for the Shaw spread now and looking for a couple of reliable ranch hands. You can't run a man outa town for that.'

'Hell, Link can't run a man outa town for any reason these days!' an anonymous voice spoke up from the crowd, getting a laugh. 'Takes too long to make up his mind!'

The lawman's petulant face flushed angrily. 'You damn lot of ingrates! I keep this town peaceable an' make it safe for your womenfolk to walk the streets!'

'Yeah — he do that, all right,' someone conceded and there were murmurings of agreement. 'Long as he don't have to get outta his chair too often!'

Waterman scowled, looked hard at Durango. 'You make trouble, I'll come down on you like a fallin' tree!'

'I'll watch my step, Sheriff,' Durango said, willing to allow the lawman the final word if the man felt it put him in the right light with the townsfolk, most of whom seemed to hold him in varying degrees of contempt. 'I'm not hunting trouble.'

'You got more sense than I allowed, then!'

Durango stalled his horse, placed Della's small foodstuff and gear order at the general store, then went to the Twin Fork Saloon on the corner of Main and Custer Street. The place was well patronized for this time of the day and most of the men in the smoky bar-room were watching the batwings as the gunfighter entered. A sudden silence . . .

He walked to the bar and ordered a whiskey and a beer and while the 'keep was getting the drinks, leaned an elbow on the zinc edge facing the room.

'Della Shaw needs two ranch hands. Usual pay, and I'm here to tell you she's a better cook than you'll find in a Cheyenne hotel. I'll buy a drink for any man who wants to step up and talk it over.'

A couple of near-drunks staggered up, looking for the free drinks, but a hard look from Durango with a slight motion of his right hand dropping closer to his gun butt made them change their minds, pronto, and return to their table.

He had tossed down the whiskey and

was halfway through his beer when someone tapped him tentatively on the shoulder. Beer glass in his left hand, he glanced at the spotted and cracked mirror behind the bar, saw two strangers in worn, trail-grimed range clothes behind him. He turned slowly, right hand easing closer to his gun butt. They looked like saddle-tramps down on their luck.

'What is it, gents?'

One was a man in his forties, red-eyed and grizzled, with big calloused lands and one shoulder higher than the other. The second was younger by about ten years, tanned the colour of a rifle butt — or maybe there was a touch of Indian in there somewhere. He was lean as a broomstick but Durango had the impression that it was all sinew and ridged muscle under those trail-worn clothes.

'Might take you up on that ranch offer,' the older man said. 'Me and my sidekick here. He's Waco and I'm Salty.'

'When did you hit town?'

'While back. Know about you, Durango. Fact I seen you out-draw Flash Jack Keene in Dodge last year. I'll work on any spread you're ridin' for.'

Durango acknowledged that with a nod. He glanced at Waco. 'You?'

'I ain't never seen you before last night when you busted a few caps on them snakes tried to nail you. If you're OK with Salty, it's OK with me.'

Durango flicked his gaze from one to the other. 'You know about the local trouble?'

'Hell, yeah. First thing we learned when we hit town,' Salty said. *Were those reddened eyes those of a boozer?*

'Couple of hands working for Della Shaw were beat-up pretty bad not long ago,' Durango spelled it out.

Salty smiled, showing gapped and broken teeth. 'You tryin' to scare us off? We've seen a coupla range wars. Don't like 'em but they be a fact of life in the West. An' like I said, if you're ridin' for the spread, I guess that means protection for whoever else is workin' there.'

Waco nodded and Durango grinned. 'Step up and name your poison, gents . . . '

Waco and Salty breasted the bar alongside Durango and ordered whiskey with beer chasers. Durango paid and watched Salty down his, fast. They spoke quietly while the rest of the bar watched — and seemed to be waiting for something. A couple of men left quietly.

But nothing had happened by the time the three men went out through the batwings together. Durango turned to them. 'Go get your mounts and spares. If you need tobacco or a new shirt, tell the man in the general store I'll be along to pay for 'em when I pick up Miss Shaw's order.'

They went off obviously pleased and Durango paused to light a cigarillo. He seemed casual but there was an expectancy in him and his gaze was restless, watching everything within sight on the street.

Then three riders came out of Custer

Street, dismounted and tied their reins to the hitch rails. A very tall man and two men of average height.

Durango nodded to himself: his hunch that he wouldn't leave town without some kind of trouble had been right.

The tall man — he was about six feet five or six, weighed 200 pounds at least — stepped up on to the boardwalk, stood hipshot and thumbed back his hat. 'When they first told me you'd hit this valley, I figured you must be after me and I even thought about runnin'. Then I said to myself, 'To hell with that, Nebraska, why should you run? You got all the important folk in the valley backin' you now. Why let one lousy gunfighter drive you away from a place you're happy in?'' The tall man grinned tightly. 'How's the back, Durango?'

'Gives me hell when it rains and in the winter,' Durango said easily. 'But that's OK — makes sure I remember the yeller snake who put the bullet there.'

Nebraska's grin didn't fade even a tad. 'So that's how it's gonna be? No good you tryin' to face me down — I won't draw agin you. I know I couldn't beat you with a Texas twister in my gun arm — and if you shoot me down, you'll hang. Good ol' Link'll see to that.'

'Link and your important friends, huh?'

'You better believe it. Ask me and I'd say you're between a rock an' a hard place, mister.'

'Been there before. But I reckon I see it now, Nebraska. My gun has most everyone buffaloed around here. You try to backshoot me again and good ol' Link'll come down on you like a falling tree — believe that's an expression he favours. So you make sure everyone here on the street knows we aren't friends and that you don't aim to try to out-draw me. But you're a man who likes to use his fists. You're pretty good at it, being big and scary, to some folk. So, you figure you'll whip me in front of the town, in a knockdown, dragout, fistfight and make youself look good.'

Nebraska shrugged, still grinning. 'I've beat in a lotta heads an' ribs since last we met, Durango! You'd be a damn fool to start anythin' with me.'

Durango saw how it was meant to go: get him riled so he started things, just in case Waterman was gutsy enough to do something about it later on.

Well, Durango not only knew what was to happen, he was eager to tangle with Nebraska, had been ever since that backshot that had almost killed him.

So, knowing full well Waterman would be able to blame him afterwards — and uncaring — he flicked his burning cigarillo at Nebraska's head. As the man swiped at it and dodged, Durango took a long step forward and smashed a fist into the middle of the tall man's face.

The other two men with Nebraska got out of the way hurriedly, but the redheaded one wasn't quite fast enough and was knocked staggering by one of

Nebraska's flailing arms. Nebraska himself scuffed and swayed, finally steadying himself, putting up a hand to his face and feeling the hot blood pouring from his nose. His eyes widened in surprise — there wouldn't have been too many times in the past that he had had his nose bloodied by anyone about six inches shorter and maybe twenty-five pounds lighter. Durango was a well-built man, but he looked kind of small against Nebraska.

The man roared and came charging in, head down like a spooked buffalo, fists clenched, looking as big and hard as rocks. Durango had to move fast because Nebraska was no slouch despite his size. He stepped quickly to one side, a fist grazing his neck, and thrust out his left foot. It tangled Nebraska's tree-trunk legs and the man grunted as he went down. He hit rolling and spun onto his back, snapping his arched body like an uncoiling spring as he leapt to his feet again. He spread his arms, grinning tightly. *Look at me!*

It was an impressive move and for a moment Durango hesitated. In that pause Nebraska closed in and his arms flailed, fists hammering Durango's body, driving him back into the street. Riders and buckboards and a full-size Studebaker wagon came to a halt to watch. Men were running down the street as several voices yelled, '*Fight!*'

Link Waterman was already outside his office, starting down the steps, but checked when he saw who was brawling. He slowed, backed up onto the landing again, hard-faced as he leaned on the rails, watching.

Durango went down. Nebraska's fists suddenly changed direction from smashing into his midriff. A left caught him on the ear, turning his head for the right uppercut that hit his jaw like a cannonball in flight. Some said later his feet left the ground, others argued the claim, but in any case Durango went down — and hard.

His head buzzed and rang and lights swirled and whirled in front of his eyes.

They felt crossed and he couldn't see clearly. He sure didn't see the size fourteen boot that caved in his ribs on the left side. But he felt it and his big body skidded a yard in the dust. Nebraska sniffed and spat blood, walked forward at an easy pace, drawing his foot back, ready and eager to stomp and maim.

Durango was still dazed but instinct took over. His fingers closed over gravel and dirt and he twisted on his back — gasping with the pain it caused him — and tossed the gravel into Nebraska's sneering face. The big hands punched most of it aside but a little got through and stung him and his built-in reaction made him snap his head back and to one side.

Durango wasn't sure his long legs would hold him so he got to one knee and launched himself at Nebraska while the man was still dodging the gravel. He rammed a shoulder into the thick legs, wrapped an arm around and heaved upright with an audible grunt of effort. Nebraska's legs were pulled out from under him and he crashed to the street on his shoulders, raising plenty of dust. It blinded him temporarily and he didn't see the fist that Durango slammed into his jaw as he threw himself full length on the taller man. Nebraska failed to block it and for a moment thought his jaw was broken. The bone creaked and his teeth crumbled. He bit his tongue, tasting his own blood as he spat pieces of wrecked teeth.

Then Durango lifted and dropped a knee to Nebraska's barrel chest, driving the breath from him. The big man gagged, and rolled on to his side, fighting for air. Durango stood, straddling the man, grabbed his shirt and with a massive effort hauled him half-upright. Nebraska's head was loose on his shoulders but old fighting instincts took over and he stiffened his spine, closed his fists and started a couple of punches. They didn't land before Durango's right hammered down above his left eye, blinding him as the skin split and blood flowed. His own arms flailed wildly, hitting Durango, but the gunfighter was firm on his feet and he slammed his fist down again, back and forth, smashing Nebraska's head from side to side, blood and sweat flying.

'*Watch out*!'

Through the roaring in his ears, Durango heard the warning, several voices yelling at once. He dropped Nebraska instantly, stepped over him, turning — in time to see the man's two companions coming in to lend Nebraska a hand. They stopped dead as Durango's Colt appeared in his fist and then blurred in two savage arcs. One man somersaulted and spread out on his face in the dust. The other, the redhead, got his hands up to his head in time and screamed as the iron of the gun crushed his fingers against his skull. He dropped to his knees and the gunfighter kicked him all the way down with a boot in the chest.

He rammed the gun back into his

holster almost as fast as he had drawn it — and staggered as Nebraska, who had regained his breath, swung a punch into his back. He stumbled and went down to one knee. He heard Nebraska take a step forward and hurled himself to the left, the big man's boot missing his head by a whisker. He shoulder-rolled and came up under Nebraska's wildly looping punch, driving the top of his head under the other man's jaw. The sound of his already broken teeth smashing together was audible even to the cheering crowd. Blood appeared on Nebraska's crushed lips; more broken teeth sparkled briefly in the sunlight.

Durango stepped in, sank a fist to the wrist in the man's relaxed midriff and when he doubled up, retching, lifted a knee into that mauled face.

Big as he was, Nebraska flew backwards, arms flailing like a wounded bird's wings, long hair flying briefly, as he crashed on to his back in the dust that rose as if a horse had fallen.

Durango stumbled to one knee,

putting down one hand to steady himself — not his gun hand, even at this moment . . .

He stayed there, chest heaving, sweat stinging his eyes, blood dripping from his jaw, knuckles swelling and aching. He was aware of the crowd's yells fading slowly and then a shadow crawled across the ground in front of him. Durango raised his battered face slowly, knowing full well who he was going to see.

Sheriff Link Waterman stood there with hands on his hips, staring down into the bloody face. He was even now very sober, eyes hard. Then suddenly he smiled.

'Best fight I've seen in a coon's age. It was time someone took that Nebraska down a peg or two. Glad it was you, gunfighter, 'cause you sure look as if you're sufferin'!' He looked around at the stunned crowd who had expected him to bluster and threaten Durango with arrest. 'Don't say I'm a killjoy ever again — but don't get the idea I won't break up any other fights, or crack a few heads when I figure I need to.'

The crowd remained silent a few moments and then as the sheriff stepped forward and helped Durango to his feet, someone said, 'My God! Link's finally got off'n the fence!'

Someone else said, 'Yeah — he musta fell. An' landed on his head!'

That brought laughter and animation back to the crowd but Waterman ignored it all, helped Durango to the steps where the gunfighter sat down gratefully, nodding to the sheriff.

'Get yourself cleaned up and outa my town in thirty minutes,' Waterman snapped, stepped around Durango and stomped back into his office.

Despite the pain, Durango grinned and dabbed at his bleeding mouth.

That was more like the Waterman he knew!

8

VALLEY PEOPLE

It was mighty hard to sit a saddle even two full days after the fight in Two Rivers' main street.

Durango's face looked little better than when he had been helped to the boardwalk by Link Waterman and Nebraska still lay bleeding and unconscious in the dust. Waco and Salty had escorted him back to the Shaw spread, the BDS, and an astonished Della had doctored his many cuts and bruises.

She seemed very alarmed when Salty told her it was Nebraska whom Durango had fought. She was even more surprised when Waco added that the sheriff had admitted to enjoying the brawl and even helped the gunfighter to the boardwalk.

'But he told him to git outa town in half an hour.'

Typical of Waterman, she thought, but was still puzzled that he hadn't at least tried to lock up Durango. Perhaps he really had climbed down from his fence-sitting.

'Durango, you're in more danger than ever now,' she told him, as she sewed up a cut above his right eye with regular dressmaking thread. He gritted his teeth and took a little time to answer.

'Maybe, but maybe not. Anything happens to me now, like getting shot from ambush, first man Waterman's gonna look up is Nebraska.'

'And do you think he won't have every single man on Case's Block C swear he couldn't have done it because he was working on the spread — in full view of all of them?'

He nodded gently. 'Well, I guess that's how it'd work. But I'm used to riding and watching my back at the same time.'

'Perhaps. But it didn't help you that other time when Nebraska shot you!'

He smiled crookedly. 'This time I'll know to watch out for him. Don't worry about such things, Della. I haven't been riding around this country for more than ten years without learning how to take care of myself.'

She knotted the thread and snipped it off, wiped away some blood. Her face was pale and concerned. 'Well, I'm *not* used to that kind of thing. I-I don't know that I feel quite right about this, Durango.'

'Look at it this way — I said I'd stand up for you and the homesteaders. I'll do it, whether I stay here or somewhere else. It's what Beau would expect of me and *want* me to do.'

She sighed as she cleared up the bloodstained bandages and disinfectant. 'Durango, I appreciate what you're doing, but I've never been one for violence.' He arched his eyebrows quizzically and she flushed, tight-lipped. 'It was out of character for me to attack you the way I did — but I was convinced at that time that you'd caused Beau's death.'

He was struggling into his shirt and she helped him slide his arms into the sleeves — seeing the deep, puckered scar just under his left shoulder blade. There were other, smaller scars, too, but this one was obviously the one caused by Nebraska's bullet.

'Might help if you took me round the valley so I could talk with the other homesteaders,' he said quietly and she knew he was right: this wasn't just her decision. He had offered to fight on behalf of all the homesteaders.

'You rest up tomorrow and we'll go the next day. There are plenty of chores to keep Waco and Salty busy.'

Now they were riding through a quarter-section where the land was a lot more cultivated than Della's and another holding he could see near the far slopes off to his left.

'This belongs to Bill Trevayne,' she told him, riding close alongside. 'He had his own place in Colorado, lost it to a forest fire that burned him out and killed his wife. He's married again now and determined to make a go of things.'

Durango nodded. 'Kind of men they need to open up places like this. How's he react to Dancey and Case?'

She shook her head. 'Not well. He's from Tennessee and Collier and Case are both from the north. Dancey comes from Texas originally, I think — he's more or less the leader of the trio, but doesn't have final say.'

Trevayne was a small man, a little cock-rooster packing an old Dragoon pistol that pulled at his worn leather belt around his narrow hips with its four-plus pounds of iron.

He pumped Durango's hand enthusiastically. 'An honour, suh! I only wish I'd been in town to see you whale the daylights outa that corn-shuckin' s-o-b Nebraska! You can call on me for anythin' you have a'mind where the Big Three are concerned.'

'Hoping we won't have to go up agin

'em in any kind of a confrontation, Trevayne,' Durango told him and watched the disappointment wash over the small, pinched face with its straggling moustache.

'Well, suh, we sure as Hades cain't 'llow you to do this all alone! You is standin'-up for us, an' we are duty-bound to side you in whatever you decide! Just want you to know I'm ready when you need me!'

Durango waited for the rebel yell, but it didn't come. But Bill Trevayne surely was spoiling for trouble.

The next place was run by Mort Bexley, a ball of a man with his trouser belt strained out to the last hole, his big belly seeming to push ahead of him as he waddled along. He was in his fifties and admitted this was probably his last chance to make good; he could never hope to earn enough to buy his own place working for someone else.

Bexley didn't know much about cattle and was aiming to make his place into a producing farm — which did not sit easy with the Big Three or the men who worked for them. His planted crops had suffered several times with riders from up-valley trampling them, tearing down his fences. *Goddamn sodbuster! Go plant your gardens someplace else: like in Hell!*

'I don't aim to make no trouble, mister,' he told the gunfighter in his wheezing voice. 'I'll fight if I have to, I guess, but I ain't 'zactly a fightin' man.' He tapped his more than ample belly.

'You run into any trouble, you tell me,' Durango said. 'I'll handle it.'

Bexley looked squarely at him with his watery eyes. 'I reckon you'll have to. If I could spare it, I'd kick in some money but I can't even do that. I tell you, I'm lookin' for peace. I don't 'zactly go along with your style — no offence, but I ain't sure you sidin' us homesteaders is really a good thing. Might make more trouble than we need.'

'Well, that's up to you, Mr Bexley, but I'm here on your behalf and money's not a part of this,' Durango said crisply and, later, when they had cleared Bexley's land, he said to Della, 'For a man who figures this is his last chance at security, he doesn't seem to want to do much about it.'

'His wife's ill — that's why he didn't invite us in. He's a very private man, and, perhaps surprisingly, a very devoted husband and father.'

'He's got kids, too! Why the hell isn't he prepared to fight harder then?'

'He's not a coward, if that's what you're thinking. He's just a man who treads softly. He loves his family, and knows that if anything happens to him, they'd have no one. He'd rather be called a quitter and move on with his family intact and try to start over someplace else.'

Durango shook his head. 'Never find what they want, that kind. Oh, I admire the devoted family man part, but not fighting tooth-and-nail for 'em — well, it don't sit right.'

'Not with you — from what I know,

you've had to fight one way or another all your life.' He snapped his head around and she smiled as he winced. 'You know Beau looked on you as his hero: he made it his business to find out everything he could about you. I probably know as much about you as you know about yourself.'

'And we're still friends?'

For a moment she was startled, then realized he meant it as a joke and she laughed as he smiled, too.

The third homesteader at the foot of the range was Tim O'Hagen, a wild-eyed, bearded Irishman who liked to play the fiddle. Della told Durango the man had a moonshine still somewhere out the back of his place and warned him not to mention it. He made more money from selling his whiskey than he did from farming or cattle. Which maybe accounted for the rundown, underdeveloped look of the place.

'So you're the boyo who nearly did for that rascal Nebraska.' He was lean and bony with a sharp face and a prominent nose. ''Tis a pity you never teased the dirty dog enough to make him go for his gun — then he would be dead, if I have my facts right about you.'

His querying glance was for Della and she nodded soberly. 'I think you have the right facts, Tim. Durango is the fastest gun in this neck of the woods. If not the whole of the Territory.'

'Ah, well, then — you must know what ye're about, boyo, but I'm thinkin' it would've been better if you'd killed yon Nebraska. Better for all of us, but specially yeself.'

'I'll have to kill him some day,' Durango said. 'I'm ready to go up against Dancey and his friends, but there might be a time I need extra help — can I count on you?'

'An' me born within a shillelagh's throw of Fingal's Cave? An' me dear mither an' fayther, God rest their souls, both from County Down . . . ?' The accent was deliberately exaggerated.

'I withdraw the question,' Durango said, with a faint smile.

Tim O'Hagen seemed a trifle suspicious, but decided that Durango wasn't joshing him, leaned closer, spoke in a harsh whisper. 'Be best, boyo, if we seal the deal with a little Irish dew. 'Tis good for what ails you and I can see that what ails you cain't be anywhere near as bad as what ails Nebraska, seein' as you won the fight — tho' I have to say when I first saw you, I thought you musta lost.'

Durango smiled wider and grimaced as the movement of his lips cracked open some of the splits. 'Appearances are sometimes deceiving, Mr O'Hagen.'

'That be very true, Mr Durango. Er — Miss Della, are ye kind of partial to . . . ?' He made a short drinking motion with one of his knobbly hands up near his mouth.

Della shook her head swiftly. 'I believe I'll settle for a sip of buttermilk, if you have any, Tim.'

‘Ah, ’tis a wise gel ye be, a very wise gel.’

* * *

Riding towards the next homesteader’s, Della asked, ‘Well, what do you think? We’re a motley lot, aren’t we?’

‘That’s for sure — but you’re the underdogs and that’s who I’m sworn to protect.’

‘Sworn? Who to . . . ?’

He said nothing and after a short time she nodded as they waded their horses across a creek, and said half-aloud,

‘You’ve sworn it to yourself! I should’ve known that . . . ’

* * *

Jason Case glared at Nebraska as the big man swilled a mouthful of rotgut and retained the fiery liquid before swallowing. He put a hand to his battered face and moaned.

'Jesus, Boss. I'll have to go see the goddamn dentist! That son of a bitch Durango smashed half my blamed teeth! Tongue's all cut, cheeks, too. Can't sleep for the pain an' whatever I'm swallowin' makes me sick!' He kicked at the rough but sturdy bunk-house straightback chair and it skidded over the uneven floor to bounce off the corner of the deal table. Still swearing, Nebraska leaned down and massaged his foot.

'You're a damn fool. You should've finished the job you didn't do properly before.' Case had no sympathy for his foreman. He was a medium-sized man, nudging 45, with close-set gimlet eyes that made everyone he met writhe uncomfortably. *Case-hardened*, folk said about those eyes.

'Finished him how?' Nebraska put a hand to his mouth. His jaw ached when he spoke above a whisper. 'Waterman was standin' by. I figured it'd make him look bad if I beat him with my fists — '

'But you *didn't* beat him. You look

like you've been run over by a freight train. You're the one came out lookin' stupid.'

Nebraska wasn't afraid of Case, not like most of the men who worked for him. He had been with the rancher for too long, knew too much about him, for that. 'OK, OK! I tried and I feel worse than stupid! I feel downright miserable. But I've made up my mind: I'm gonna see that damn tooth-puller.'

'Then go — get it done and be back here by supper time! I'm meetin' with Dancey and Collier tonight and I want you with me.'

'Judas! After spendin' the afternoon in a dentist's chair?'

Case lifted a thick finger to within inches of Nebraska's reddened eyes. 'You . . . be . . . back . . . by the time I said!'

He turned and strode out of the bunkhouse, and Nebraska consoled himself with the thought that any of the luckless cowpokes working the ranch yard need only make some minor mistake now and they would have the hide torn off them by Case's tongue in his present mood.

The man was right though: he should've killed that bastard Durango. Somehow.

Well, maybe he'd give some thought to putting that to rights pretty damn soon! *There had to be some way* . . .

He moaned softly to himself as he gently — very gently — massaged his tender jaw. He had trouble even chewing bread he'd dipped in his coffee — and Nebraska was a man who liked plenty of meat in his diet, half-raw preferred.

The big ramrod saddled his horse and mounted, but before he had cleared the ranch, he knew he should have taken time to hitch up a buckboard. The jarring of each step his mount took ran clear up into the top of his head — via his smashed mouth.

By the time he had reached town he was almost incoherent with rage at the pain and headed straight for the saloon.

Men cleared a space for him as he growled his way to the bar, thumped one giant fist on the counter.

'Whiskey! Plenny goddamned — whiskey!' He moaned and swayed, suddenly clutching his jaw. '*Chris'sakes hurry*!'

Two men a few feet away nudged each other and winked: they knew Nebraska was in great pain, and they knew why. 'Durango,' one man whispered to the other who nodded.

But it was loud enough for Nebraska to hear and he wrenched around, eyes wide, bloody mouth twisted as he raised his giant arms and descended on the two drinkers.

In full white-face panic now, they turned and tried to run. But massive fingers clawed deep into their shoulders and they were lifted clear of the floor so fast their feet were still moving in mid-air.

But not for long. Nebraska growled like a bear and smashed their heads together, knocking them senseless. He looked at the two limp things in his hands and flung them aside, scattering other drinkers, the unconscious men skidding and knocking over tables and chairs.

Then he turned back to the bar where the 'keep was pouring a shotglass of whiskey with a shaking hand. Nebraska sent the small glass flying, grabbed the bottle from the unprotesting barman and tilted his head back mouth open.

He lifted the bottle and let a thick stream pour between his battered lips, thinking, *I gotta kill that son of a bitch Durango, I just gotta!*

9

WANTED DEAD

The Big Three all wanted Durango dead.

Strangely enough, Big John Dancey seemed to be the only one who wasn't absolutely sure.

'What's stickin' in your craw, John?' asked Case in his grating voice. 'Figured you'd be all for it.'

'Yeah, me, too,' chipped in Brant Collier, looking puzzled, though he hadn't been particularly enthusiastic.

Dancey met both their gazes squarely enough. 'I dunno — just a feelin'. Somethin' about that gunfighter. He's deadly as they come but . . . he just don't seem to be the cold-blooded killer that, say, someone like John Wesley Hardin is, or Clay Allison. Sure, he'll nail his man before a gnat can blink;

but you think back and you'll find that anyone he's killed has been tryin' to kill him.'

Case spread his arms in a 'so what?' gesture.

'Well, Clay Allison'd bust a cap on anyone who looked at him sideways, had he the notion at that moment, and that's man, woman or child.'

'Ah, it's when he's drunk Clay goes kinda crazy,' Collier allowed, 'but I wouldn't want to be around him whether he was s'posed to be on our side or not.'

'Well, you won't have to worry about that,' Case growled. 'Big John, we gotta get this done. I know a little about Durango, seen him in the Black Hills one time when there was that fracas between the miners and the cow-men — '

'You *seen* him?' cut in Dancey, and his query brought more puzzlement to Collier's face, too. 'When was you there? Must've been before you came here.'

'Well, maybe I shouldn't've said 'seen' him,' Case said obviously trying a mite too late to cover up a slip. 'But I had a feller workin' for me who'd been there and he told me that Durango whipped up them miners without even tryin' and organized 'em into standin' ground agin the cattlemen. They'd've followed the son of a bitch anywhere, right up to the doors of Hell itself — accordin' to my ranch hand.'

'Who was that, Case?' Dancey asked, trying to look and sound innocently interested, but Case scowled: he knew Big John was cynical of the story and he cursed himself for that slip of the lip.

Dancey was smart enough to start putting things together if he thought about it: Case's absence from Killdeer Valley for several weeks at the time of the Black Hills' troubles; the rumours about the assay office being robbed of its stocks of gold dust and nuggets by an outsider . . .

'Thing is,' Case said, ignoring

Dancey's question now, 'we're gonna have to pay to have it done and that means us three've got to cough up the *dinero*.'

'Well, don't look at me. I've got a damn lot of beef to replace after that stampede last month. And I'm still not convinced it wasn't started by one of them damn sodbusters! That crazy Irishman, I favour. Now I'm gonna have to look to the bank for a loan.' Dancey almost spat, he was so annoyed. He let his words hang, but if the others figured he was hinting they might finance him, they didn't react.

'What about your man, Nebraska, Jace?' Collier asked quickly: everyone knew he was tight with a dollar. 'He's got scores to settle with Durango. Give him a hundred bucks and he'll do it, won't he?'

'Not right now he won't. Anyway, he don't work that cheap, and Waterman's got him in the jailhouse, anyway.' Of course, Dancey and Collier wanted to know why. Case sighed. 'Durango smashed up his mouth good in that brawl, so Nebraska decided to go see the dentist. Took on a bellyful of redeye first an' busted up the saloon. Then the dentist apparently gave him some kind of stuff to put him out so's he wouldn't feel the pain.' He shrugged. 'Didn't mix with the whiskey too good — Nebraska went berserk and threw the dentist out of the window.'

'Judas priest! The dentist's rooms're upstairs above Clancy's barber shop!' breathed Collier. Case nodded.

'Right now he's in the infirmary nursing a broken arm and a busted ankle, some cracked ribs and a slew of cuts from the glass. Waterman caught Nebraska on the hop, managed to bend a gun barrel over his head the way he does with drunks, knocked him out and dragged him off to jail.'

'Bail him out,' Dancey said, also favouring the bitter-faced giant ramrod for the job of killing Durango. He was mighty short of money, didn't aim to spend any to buy the murder of the gunfighter if he could help it.

'Well, I could go see Link, I guess,' Case allowed slowly. 'He might let me bail Nebraska — but somethin' happens to that gunfighter and he'll go lookin' for Nebraska anyway.'

'Hell, give him an extra fifty, send him to the Prime Cut in Cheyenne for a week right after he does the job.'

Case looked bleakly at Dancey, then Collier. 'You two damn pikers! Don't think past your wallets, do you?' He tapped himself on the chest. 'I need Nebraska! I don't want to get rid of him. He stays with me. No, we'll have to find some other way to take care of that gunhawk.'

'Or give Waterman somethin' else to think about so's he won't put Nebraska at the top of his suspect list,' Big John Dancey said slowly.

Both the others looked towards him and slowly they all smiled.

They liked the idea.

* * *

'Nebraska's out!'

Waco announced the news as he dismounted in the yard of the BDS ranch, a little breathless. Durango was riveting on a new spur rowel that had kept him busy for an hour or so and he hit his thumb with the hammer and smothered a curse.

'How'd that happen? Thought the dentist was screaming he was gonna charge him with assault and hell knows what else.'

'Seems Case talked Waterman around into lettin' him bail him out in his custody, said he was needed at the ranch.'

The voices brought Della to the door, holding an oven cloth, flour dusting her hands and forearms. 'What's Nebraska's mood?' she asked quietly.

Waco shrugged. 'Headed straight for the saloon. I went as far as the batwings, caught the look on his face in the bar mirror, then went about my — your business, Miz Shaw.'

She smiled. 'I think that was probably the wisest thing to do, Waco. Salty on his way back from town?'

'Drivin' the buckboard back with the fencin' wire but the store couldn't fill all the order. Supplies're short because of the floods up north. Both rivers are up.'

'This might mean those three land-grabbers have something in the wind, Della,' Durango said, giving the rowel rivet one final tap with the hammer. He fitted the straps as he spoke, buckling the spur into place on his boot. 'Nebraska seems to be the big man where the rough stuff's concerned and he's likely in one helluva mood with his teeth still busted and having been gunwhipped silly by Link Waterman. That wouldn't set too easy with a man like him: Waterman's only half his size. Be a good time for Case and the others to stir him up and turn him loose on the homesteaders.'

Della was alarmed, seeing the sense of this, knowing from the past that it was just the kind of thing the Big Three would do.

'You could be right, but I'm not sure Case would want to sacrifice Nebraska: they seem closer than usual for rancher and range boss.' She flicked her eyes to Durango. 'Still: they never had you to contend with before and they might try to bait you by doing something . . . rough, to see just how far you'll go.'

'Well, they'll find out. Waco, you want to ride and warn the other homesteaders there could be trouble brewing?'

'Sure. Just gimme time to change my hoss.'

'You can take time for some coffee and biscuits first,' Della said going back into the house.

Waco grinned. 'I surely can, ma'am!'

* * *

Nothing happened that night and the word was that Case had gotten Nebraska out of town before he took on a load of redeye and stoked up his temper.

Link Waterman was said to have laid it on the line with Case: keep a tight rein on Nebraska, or next time he put him in jail, he'd throw away the key.

'Link seems to be finding his own two feet,' Durango opined and Della agreed.

'It's about time. I don't think he's as scared as most folk believe. It's just that he's a man who does as little as necessary, trying to please everyone. It never works out successfully for anybody, that sort of thing.'

Durango agreed. 'That's for sure.'

Salty had smuggled in a jug of whiskey when he brought in the supplies in the buckboard and when it was his turn to stay in the barn and watch for signs of aggression in the valley two nights later, he got his bottle from the bottom of a grain bin and took a swig or two.

Which became three or four — and more . . .

Next morning when Durango and Waco awoke in the small bunkhouse and went to the washbench to clean up before breakfast, empty corrals stared them in the face.

'What the hell!' breathed Durango, looking in all directions, shivering a little in the early wind. But there wasn't a single horse to be seen.

Della had only had a small remuda — about a dozen mounts — and one of the chores coming up was for Durango, Salty and Waco to start trapping mustangs in the hills and bring down a bunch for breaking-in.

Waco knew what had happened: he had had a swig or two of the smuggled whiskey the night he was on watch. But he knew his old pard Salty would've had trouble stopping at just a couple of snorts.

They found Salty snoring on some hay, reeking of booze, the empty bottle lying on the ground near his fingertips. Durango was rough with him, bunched up his shirt front and shook the man till

Waco was afraid his pard's rocking head would snap his scrawny neck. Salty moaned and groaned. Durango leapt back as the man was violently sick.

Swearing, the gunfighter dragged him out to the horse trough and dumped him in bodily. The commotion brought Della into the yard and she ran halfway down towards the horse trough before it dawned on her the corrals were empty.

'What — what's happened?' she asked as Durango dragged the half-drowned Salty over the edge of the trough and dumped him to flounder on the wet ground.

'This fool had a jug of whiskey, drank himself stupid and let someone steal the remuda! Damn you, Salty! I've had that buckskin for years! If anything's happened to him I'll take it out of your lousy hide.'

Salty was feeling mighty sorry for himself by this time, tried a few mumbling explanations but Durango grew impatient, rounded on the silent, worried-looking Waco.

'He's your pard. Get him cleaned up and then we'll start looking for the horses.'

'Judas! On foot!' Waco exclaimed.

'How else?' Durango growled, and then said to Della, 'unless one of us can walk over to Trevayne's and borrow some mounts . . .?'

'Yes, Bill will oblige, I'm sure.' Della started looking towards the ridge that hid Trevayne's spread from hers and then stiffened. 'I . . . thought that was dust, stirred up by the wind! But do you smell smoke?'

Durango did and Waco, too. Salty was still trying to stay on his feet, head hanging.

'Oh, dear Lord,' Della said, clutching the wooden batter spoon she held much more tightly to her bosom as she studied that thin greyish cloud hanging above the ridge.

Durango turned to Waco and the sorry-looking Salty.

'Get your guns,' he said grimly.

* * *

The night before, over the ridge, at Trevayne's place, Bill Trevayne heard the riders coming across the ford long before they started up the gentle incline to where his cabin stood. He was a light sleeper at the best of times and since speaking with that gunfighter he had been sleeping more lightly than ever.

His wife was wheezing with her ailing lungs and the two kids, both girls, were relaxed in the deep sleep of innocence in their corner behind the strung Indian blanket.

He slid out of bed, reaching for the shotgun on the floor, taking the big Dragoon sixgun as well, in its holster rig and cartridge belt from where it hung on the bed post.

He got as far as the door and then they came into the yard with a rush, whooping like Indians, yelling madly, hoping to scare the pants off the Trevayne family. Bill swore softly, wrenched the door open, stepping outside and putting his back against the log wall. Behind him he heard a tremulous query from one of the girls, young Daisy, he reckoned.

Then the first of the three raiders came thundering past, guns hammering, shooting the tin chimney full of holes, smashing in the only window that had glass panes, tearing white streaks in the logs, bark and splinters flying. Bill was down on one knee, triggered the shotgun, but nothing happened and he flung it aside, cursing himself for trying to save pennies by using those years-old cartridges he had unearthed in an old clothes trunk.

His big Dragoon thundered, and the huge flash gave away his position.

'Hey! The lousy Reb's puttin' up a fight!' Bill knew that stentorian voice: it could only belong to Nebraska.

He fired towards it but three guns trained on his muzzle flash and he was smashed on to his back. Bleeding and fighting to stay alive for as long as possible, he brought his gun across his body, using both shaking hands, saw a rider standing in the stirrups, rifle going to shoulder. Bill got off one more shot and lived just long enough to see his bullet had failed to knock the raider out of the saddle, but not long enough to hear the first scream from his young daughters and the gargling sound of his wife trying to call his name . . .

Later the same night at Bexley's spread where the rise and fall of hills and ridges deadened the sounds of gunfire, Mort Bexley, next down the homesteader line, didn't have a notion anything was amiss.

The first he knew was when they dropped a stick of dynamite down his well and water geysered and rock chips pattered against the wall and roof of the cabin.

In his nightshirt, big belly pushing out ahead of him, he rushed to the door, reaching with one hand for the rifle he kept above it on a pair of nails, the other flicking up the latch. For a man of his bulk and one whose heart was hammering and leaping wildly in fright, he did all right. The door slammed open and the rifle crashed in a series of fast shots, mostly unaimed.

He couldn't see too well in the dark but there was nothing wrong with his hearing. He fired at hoofbeats as they drew closer, instinctively chose the moment they were nearest, and then triggered and levered two or three shots. He heard at least one man yell in pain — then two bullets slammed into his body, spun it so that he fell half-in and half-out of the cabin, across the threshhold.

His wife screamed, trembling hands covering her ears under her wildly flying hair. A child sobbed hysterically . . .

At O'Hagen's . . . twenty minutes later, there was no Luck of the Irish for Tim O'Hagen.

He didn't know about the raids on the other spreads, but he knew about the one on his own fast enough.

Someone located his still and blew it

up, the thunderous explosion spilling him out of bed. He saw the red flash of the flames and, staggering a little from the liquor he had drunk earlier, grabbed his old Spencer carbine and stumbled out the back door.

'Ah, the little Irishman himself!' a deep voice bellowed. 'Well, now, you remember that time you wouldn't gimme a jug of your lousy rotgut 'cause I was broke? Even when I promised to pay when I got my wages? You wouldn't take my word. If you've forgot, I ain't. Time to pay the piper, O'Hagen!'

O'Hagen knew it was Nebraska and his belly cringed despite the fortifying Irish dew screaming through his veins. 'An' ye'll get none of me brew this night, neither, you great lump of dog's vomit!'

Nebraska's deep belly laugh surprised him. He could now see the big man's face in the flames coming from the burning brush where the still had been.

'That I won't, you son of a bitch!

Now go on back to your painted ancestors in the peat bogs!’

Nebraska’s gun hammered a brief burst and Tim O’Hagen twisted and danced and finally fell, tumbling off his back porch in an untidy, broken-looking heap.

‘Right, boys!’ Nebraska yelled. ‘Burn that stinkin’ hovel and let’s get on — we got a couple of other visits to make before this night’s over!’

10

MAN BEHIND THE STAR

It was well past noon when they stumbled in to the charred remains of Bill Trevayne's place.

There were others there before them: armed men from town, led by Sheriff Link Waterman. He was grimed with soot and charcoal, his clothes dirty. He regarded the walking newcomers from across the ridge soberly.

'Mrs Trevayne somehow made it to the swing-station at Carver's Bend,' Waterman said without preamble. 'With her lungs she wasn't up to climbin' the ridge to see if you folk could help — but I guess you wouldn't've anyway, comin' in afoot.'

It was a long way round of asking how come no mounts and it didn't impress Durango. But Della, reading his tight face, placed a hand on his arm and, still breathless from the climb and long walk, said, 'Someone stole our horses during the night, Link. We saw smoke this morning and walked over the ridge.'

'In other words, you weren't raided!' the sheriff said grimly.

She shook her head, glanced around at the gathered men. 'Where's Lucy Trevayne now?'

'One of the stage wranglers took her into town to Doc Mayfield,' a townsman answered. 'She looked mighty poorly to me, Della.'

'Who did this, Sheriff?' asked Durango.

'You dunno?'

Durango was immediately wary: he had run up against a hundred lawmen in his time and whenever they answered a question with a question he knew they were looking for answers themselves and anyone even remotely suspicious was in for a hard time. 'How would I know? I was asleep and there's a whole damn ridge between us and this place.'

'But you can see down valley pretty well.'

Durango frowned. 'So . . . ?'

'So no one noticed any fires, heard any shootin' or explosions?' Link Waterman's face was tightening by the minute now as Durango shook his head briefly. 'No one was thinkin' there could be trouble a'brewin' in the valley?'

Durango spoke slowly. 'Everyone knows trouble's been brewing for a long time. Why last night more than any other?'

Della was hanging on Link's answer as eagerly as Durango and the others.

'Because that was the word goin' around town — that the valley was ready to explode.'

'I don't see how that could be,' Della Shaw said sharply, searchingly. 'There's been tension for a long time, but I know of nothing that could bring it to a head like this. Who started such talk?'

'Who knows? These things just seem to happen.'

'And you did nothing about it?' Durango asked, earning a bleak look from the lawman. 'Just waited to see . . . ?'

'Wasn't enough to do anythin' — but there sure as hell is now. Trevayne's dead. Bexley's barely alive and that boozy Irishman way down the end is dead as a toad. McGuinness and Callaghan had their places shot up, too, herds run over a cliff. Their ranch hands have quit and lit-out.'

'Dear God!' breathed Della. She looked bewilderedly at Durango. 'They're cleaning out the valley!'

'All that's happened, and you make a veiled accusation that we might know something about it?' the gunfighter said to the sheriff, grim-faced.

Waterman wasn't fazed. 'I sent a man up the ridge earlier to see if your place had been raided, too, and he said no, hadn't been touched, looked just as usual. Except there were no horses.'

He glared around at Durango, the girl and the two ranch hands, Salty at last starting to sit up and take notice.

'That was my fault, the hosses,' Salty grated. 'I got drunk when I was s'posed to be on watch.'

Link tensed. 'On watch for what?'

Salty looked appealingly at Durango who said, 'We heard you'd released Nebraska. He still has it in for me after that fight. I thought he might be stupid enough to try something. And I'd say he did just that.'

Waterman snorted. 'He might be that stupid, but Case ain't — nor is Dancey, nor Collier. They tread easy, these days. You're kinda jumpin' at shadows, ain't you, gunfighter?'

'It's a way of staying alive.'

'Or coverin' up.'

'Covering up what?'

'Your intentions.'

'You think I made those raids?' Durango was incredulous that the lawman could be so booby-headed about this, but Waterman shook his head slowly.

'Not alone, no. I been doin' some

readin' on you, gunfighter. You was in a range war, few years back, in South Dakota. Seems both sides was leery of you, even the one who hired you: cattlemen, weren't it? You brung in men from the hills — men dodgin' the law for one reason or another — an you led them on a raid on *both* camps, ranches *and* miners. They blamed each other and were ready for an all-out shootin' war, but good sense prevailed and they ended up workin' out a solution to their problems.'

Della was staring hard at Durango and he nodded slightly, admitting it was true. 'Just showed 'em what could happen: that there wouldn't be any winner. They'd both lose too much to claim a victory.'

'My God, that was drastic!' Della breathed, but Durango just shrugged.

'It worked. Both sides were ruthless and greedy — they needed shaking up.'

She was still staring at him thoughtfully when Waterman scowled.

'Well, you ain't gonna get away with

usin' them kinda tactics in my bailiwick, mister! Fast gun or no.'

'I didn't raid anyone last night — and no one got killed in that Dakota deal, Sheriff. There were wounded and a lot of propety got damaged or destroyed, but that was only to underline what I was trying to show 'em. You read that far in your research?'

It was plain by the look on Waterman's face that he hadn't read about that part but he chose to ignore the question and said, 'That touch of runnin' off Della's hosses was nice: no hosses, so no raid, huh? Guess you did it after the raids. Then what happened? You hide 'em back in the hills someplace? Aim to collect 'em later?'

'You're plumb loco, Waterman,' the gunfighter said and Della tensed as she heard the steely edge to his words. He was being pushed too far, but Waterman seemed too boneheaded to notice. 'You're not even listening to me.'

'But there was one problem, wasn't

there?' the sheriff pressed on, tight-lipped now, sweating a little. 'Your buckskin got shot! An' now he's lyin' out at the Irishman's — feeding the vultures, I'd reckon.'

Della dug her fingers into Durango's arm. Salty licked his lips and kind of edged behind Waco. Durango's gaze burned into the lawman.

'Buck's dead? Out at O'Hagen's?'

'Yeah — where he fell. Dunno what you planned to do about him, but I got there ahead of you. An' now I s'pose you're gonna tell me you weren't ridin' the buckskin, that you was tucked up nice an' snug in your bed on the Shaw place while raiders blew up O'Hagen's still and burned his cabin after killin' him?'

'You're trying too hard to frame me for this, Waterman.' Della knew Durango was deliberately fighting to stay cool, but she was afraid he might lose patience with the stubborn sheriff and — well, she didn't know what might happen. 'Someone put a bug in your ear?'

Abruptly, surprising herself even, Della said, 'Your accusations are totally absurd, Link!' All eyes turned to her as she spoke directly to the now wary lawman. 'I can swear that Durango never left my ranch last night. He' — she hesitated briefly, then lifted her jaw and said — 'because he was with me — in my bed.'

The hush on the hillside was total. Even the birdsong seemed to stop suddenly. She clasped her hands tightly and there was a flush to her cheeks. Durango snapped his head around and said, 'You don't have to do this, Della!'

'It's done,' she breathed. 'Too late to take it back — anyway, it's no business of anyone's but ours. If it'll straighten out this . . . this really *dumb* situation, I-I don't give a damn.'

She was obviously uncomfortable with all the shocked gazes flung in her direction and the murmurings that started, even a few leers. She looked up into Durango's face and said quietly,

'Don't try to deny it — that'll only make it worse.'

He sighed. 'I wish you hadn't done that. There was no need. I could've handled it . . . '

'Perhaps, and perhaps not. I know Link Waterman. He's been out to get you ever since you arrived and he won't let go of this unless he has absolute proof that you couldn't've done this terrible thing.' She looked again at the sheriff, speaking louder. 'And, unless you want to call me a downright liar, Link, I think I've given you that proof.'

'I-I ain't callin' you a liar, Della. I'm kinda shocked, is all, but . . . '

Della didn't answer — nor did she drop her gaze. In the end the sheriff glared at the gunfighter.

'We'll leave it for now. You want to make it official an' come identify your hoss?'

'I sure as hell do!' Durango said.

* * *

He dismounted from the borrowed horse down the charred slope from the burned-out remains of O'Hagen's cabin. Beyond that, the wreckage of the hidden still made a blot on the landscape with ravaged scrub and splintered timber.

Durango stood looking down at the carcass of his once proud and loyal buckskin who had served him well for hundreds of miles over the years. He knelt and ran his hand down the cold muzzle, disturbing flies which rose in a black cloud. He stood and Link Waterman stepped back at the look on his face: it was best described as *murderous*.

Durango pointed. 'See that bullet hole in Buck's head? Smack between the eyes! The hide's singed and blackened from gunpowder! Goddamnit, Sheriff, someone put a gun muzzle against Buck's head and shot him dead where he stood!' He grabbed the sheriff's arm. 'Look at the ground around him, for Chris'sake! Not torn up or showing any sign he was running when he was shot! Look at the damn stirrups: inches longer than I'd have 'em set. It's not even my saddle.' He shook his head jerkily. 'I've never known a bigger fool than you, Waterman.'

Link Waterman jumped back. 'Now you wait a minute! I-I ain't gonna draw again you! But you cain't threaten a duly sworn lawman like that!'

'Duly sworn idiot! A blind man can see someone a lot bigger than me deliberately killed this horse, likely to settle a grudge agin me . . . now, I wonder who comes to mind?'

Waterman swallowed, face grey and tight now. 'I been to see Dancey an' the others. None of their men left the spreads last night, includin' Nebraska! He took on a load of likker in town after he was bailed, an' Case himself put him to bed. Said he slept right through till after sun-up.'

'Well, I'm glad you believe such upstanding citizens — but you had to push Della Shaw into humiliating herself in front of a lot of folk before you halfway believed my story.'

'So that's what's rilin' you — Hey! Where the hell you think you're goin'?' Waterman started to jog-trot after Durango as the man turned to mount his borrowed horse. 'This is law business! You leave it to me. I'll go see Nebraska and get the straight of this!'

Durango hesitated with one foot in the stirrup. 'Don't be a fool: he'll kill you.'

'This is my chore!' There was something a touch admirable in Waterman at that moment. Fear burned in his eyes and in his bearing. He knew he had acted dumbly — though would never admit it — and he knew how deadly Nebraska was, yet he aimed to go up against the man, trying to prove that he was a lawman who didn't shirk his duty no matter how dangerous. *Maybe he was trying to prove something to himself* . . .

Durango, shaking his head, said, 'No,

I better come with you. I've got a stake in this. Bigger'n you.'

Waterman hesitated, then shook his head. 'Nope. I mighta been a mite . . . hasty. Weakness of mine, you b'lieve some folk. I tend to make up my mind too quickly an' — well, lotsa times it turns out wrong. Then when I do get it right, it's too late. I know what folk say behind my back, so I aim to do this one myself. I don't need you. People have died here. They meant nothin' to you but I knew 'em.'

'Their *dying* wasn't your fault.'

'I let Nebraska out, so mebbe it was my fault.'

Even though he kind of admired the fumbling lawman's courage — something he hadn't suspected — Durango was sceptical, but nodded curtly. 'You get into trouble, don't be too damn proud to back down — I'll handle Nebraska.'

Waterman flushed deeply, the old quick temper flaring. 'Damn you! *Stay out of it!* By God, I'll show you and the rest of the goddamn valley! They might make fun of me but I know my duty — and I'll do it without any help from a damn gunslinger!'

Durango was surprised at Link Waterman's vehemence. The man might be stupid, but it was a kind of brave stupidity and Durango couldn't help but respect it. Then, having allotted Waterman that small portion of compassion, Durango turned and lifted a foot into the stirrup.

Maybe he'd follow at a distance, stay just out of sight, but close enough to . . .

That was all he remembered — except that something slammed across the back of his head, hard, and a roaring started in his ears as he fell into yawning blackness.

⋆ ⋆ ⋆

Dancey figured it would be best if he put in an appearance and publicly demonstrated his shock and disapproval of the raids that had virtually wiped out the homesteaders. Hooray! He took Arlo Jeffries with him, the foreman still using a stick to help him walk, although the flesh wound in his leg was healing slowly. But it was still mighty painful.

Dancey hadn't given him much sympathy, even told him he would have to pay Doc Mayfield out of his wages, adding, 'You ain't ridin' round-up in three days, you better start lookin' for another job.'

'That's a helluva thing to tell a wounded man!' But Dancey merely shrugged.

Arlo wasn't a very vindictive man, but he figured he would find a way to square things with Durango — and maybe this arrogant son of a bitch, Dancey.

'You think Durango did them raids?' he asked, as they rode into the Trevayne place, saw the milling crowd.

'I dunno — but if he did, I'd like to know who's gonna bring him in.'

Arlo sat straighter in his saddle and,

with a crooked smile, said, 'How about Link Waterman?'

'Link! Tackle someone like Durango? Don't be — ' Dancey broke off as Arlo pointed and his jaw sagged.

Coming from down-valley, Sheriff Link Waterman was leading a horse with someone slumped and roped in the saddle. They could see it was Durango, the sun glinting off his manacled hands behind his back. 'Well, smoke me!'

Dancey spurred his mount forward, followed by Arlo, the crowd moving out to meet the sheriff, Della Shaw in the fore. 'Sheriff! What's happened?' she cried.

She saw that Durango was unconscious, dark blood snaking across one side of his face from under his hairline.

The sheriff ignored Della and spoke to the group, settling his gaze on Dancey. 'Durango here's still under suspicion so I aim to lock him up. I gotta question Nebraska yet and I want this gunslinger where I can find him.'

He shifted his gaze to Arlo. 'You was my deputy before you went to ride for Big John, Arlo, you know the routine. Guess you ain't much use to Dancey right now, so, you wanna take Durango back to town for me, lock him up, and stand guard? I'll put you on full temporary pay.'

Arlo frowned, turned towards Dancey. 'You can get along without me, can't you, *boss*?' he said sardonically.

Dancey looked at Durango where Della was wiping at the blood on his face. He gave a twisted smile: it would be good to have that damn gunfighter behind bars where he could be reached . . . and couldn't fight back.

'You're right, Link. Arlo ain't much use to me right now. You figure to need him long?'

'Nope — just till I get back.'

Till he got back! Dancey kept his face sober with an effort at the sheriff's confidence. Link bracing Nebraska would be something to see, but he couldn't risk riding along just for that pleasure. *Damnit!*

'OK, Arlo, you might's well play deputy for a spell. We'll talk about your job at Circle D later.' He gave Della a half-smile. 'You can carry on without your gunfighter for a while can't you, Della?'

She glared but said nothing.

Link Waterman paused. 'Don't you go no place, Della. Nor them two fellers you got workin' for you — I just might want to talk with you again!'

Dancey chuckled. *By God! Something or someone had sure put a bee up Waterman's ass!*

11

DEAD MEN IN THE VALLEY

Jason Case was ready to kill as he glared at Nebraska. The big man seemed pleased with himself and impervious to the tongue-lashing the rancher was giving him.

'It was a stupid move! For Chris'sakes, what the hell were you thinking of to tear through the valley like that?'

Nebraska, one hip hitched over the edge of the porch rail of the ranch house, flicked his cigarette stub away and smiled crookedly, his broken teeth showing plainly.

'I was thinkin' of you. Them other two, Dancey and Collier, have been holdin' you back. What you've mostly needed to do was get rid of O'Hagen, but if you singled him out someone might've gotten suspicious and started wonderin' why . . . So, while Waterman had me in jail I got to figurin' and I reckoned why not hit the *whole damn valley*, then no one would wonder why a partic'lar sodbuster caught a dose of lead-poisonin', then we could get the you-know-what.'

Case sighed. 'Nebraska, the thought was good enough, but the timing's all wrong! Waterman's as confused and dumb as ever, but that's when he's most dangerous because you never know which way the fool's gonna jump — and that damn gunhawk, Durango, is s'posed to be on the homesteaders' side. What the hell you think he's gonna do now?'

Nebraska laughed shortly. 'He's gonna have too damn much to worry about to come after us or anyone else — I had Shep an' Luke run off Della's remuda. We hid all but three which we used on the raids so the tracks'll match if Waterman cares to look. I rode Durango's buckskin, shot it dead and left it at O'Hagen's. Once Waterman sees that he's gonna go after Durango.'

'Christ, man, that won't prove anything!'

''Course it will! Durango's hoss found dead after all them raids, on the ranch where O'Hagen was killed, his still blowed to hell? With the other tracks, too, Waterman'll nail Durango on the spot! Mebbe them ranch hands, as well; even Della, that'd get her outa your hair.'

Case was surprised at Nebraka's reasoning and planning, but — 'It *could* look bad for Durango, except for one thing: he's s'posed to be backin' the damn home-steaders! So why would he raid 'em, burn 'em out? Who would he get to help him? Even Waterman's not dumb enough to fall for that.'

'I reckon he would.' Nebraska had lost his smile now — his mouth was acting-up — and in a sullen tone he said, 'You're forgettin' Durango pulled raids on the miners and cattlemen when we was caught up in that fracas in

Dakota. *Just like this one*! We make sure Link knows about that an' he'll go after him an' he's likely to get shot if he does. Not many folk'll stand for that, even if Link is about the most cantankerous lawman ever. He's kept the town pretty much tamed down and lots of folk like him for it . . . 'kinda the devil you know'. So the whole damn' town'll be agin Durango. He'll have to quit, and when he does, I'll be waitin' along the trail as he rides out.'

'And that's what this is all about, ain't it? You want to square with Durango for beatin' the daylights outa you in front of the whole town!'

Nebraska glared. 'Damn right I do! But I don't aim to go to jail for it. There won't even be a lawman in the valley by that time, so we can go up to O'Hagen's whenever we want and no one'll care what we do up there.' He flicked a cold look at his boss. 'That's what I was thinkin' of and I 'spected you'd be a damn sight more grateful!'

Case was silent a spell, building a

cigarette. Most times, Nebraska was a man who reacted without thinking and if he was riled enough he would shoot down Case himself and worry about it afterwards. So the rancher needed to tread a mite more softly here . . .

He looked out over his ranch yard, the big barn, the corrals and milling horses, the bunkhouse, entrance to the root cellar and, beyond, to the wide flat stretch of Killdeer Valley where the rivers meandered and his cattle grazed and roamed free — *except* for where the homesteaders were moving in to the north! *But this was his place!* He'd chosen to settle here: he'd risked a helluva lot to do it but now he had the means to achieve his dream — thanks to Nebraska!

He actually jumped slightly as the realization hit home: 'Thanks to Nebraska!' *He was beholden to his ramrod! Incredible! And not so easy to take, but* — 'Nebraska, I believe there is a chance things just might work out the way you planned after all — with Waterman's pig-headedness and the loco way he thinks, *and* with a little modification here and there, we just might pull it off!'

Although it hurt, Nebraska managed a smile: he liked that 'we'.

* * *

But that wasn't the way Big John Dancey saw it. Nor did Brant Collier. In fact, Collier went into a bit of a funk, set out for Dancey's place, all shook up, and met the rancher on the way over to see him after visiting the Trevayne place.

'You've heard the news, of course!' Collier said breathlessly. 'My God! It has to've been Nebraska tryin' to frame Durango, but would Case have OK'd it?'

'I dunno, but it's sure set the cat among the pigeons,' Dancey said. 'I saw Link, but he's all at sixes and sevens as usual, tryin' to make up his mind. We have to talk with Case.'

Collier frowned. 'Well, I-I don't know as I want to be associated with Case right now. I mean, Waterman'll blame us all for this and we had nothing to do with it . . . ' He trailed off, suddenly looking suspiciously at Dancey. 'You didn't know it was going to happen, did you?'

'Hell, no! It's the last thing we needed right now. Later, maybe, but not just yet. The railroad's stressed over and over that they won't stand for outright killin'. A few beatings and so on, tear down some fences, OK. If that don't work they'll go find themselves somewhere else to build and we'll miss out. I've worked too damn hard to get them in here to see it all blow up in my face.'

Collier's frown deepened, seeing Dancey was truly riled. 'What — what're you going to do, John?'

'Square up to Case. I dunno that he knew about them raids. I don't think he'd go along with it, but he's gotta do somethin' about that maniac Nebraska! And throwin' him to the wolves is the only way as I see it. The railroad people'll demand that someone's head rolls or they're out.'

'What about the town? You can't figure the people there — some are for the homesteaders, specially the business folk, 'cause they know there'll be families that need feeding and clothes and all the other things. The railroad will bring trade, too, of course, but most folk figure the sodbusters are here to stay because they're on government land.'

'*Territorial* Gov'ment, not Federal,' Dancey pointed out. 'A powerful railroad can get around that once the settlers move out — decide they can't make a go of it.' Dancey winked, then sobered. 'But killin' 'em and burnin' 'em out won't wash. There'll be hell to pay.'

Collier nodded, looked uneasy as he said hesitantly, 'Well, I figure I might just . . . drop out, John.'

Dancey's head snapped up. 'Drop out? Of what?'

'The alliance. It's too dangerous now! We may not be a state yet, but I'll bet a federal marshal turns up here soon, and I don't want to tangle with one of them.'

Dancey noted Collier's obvious fear and wondered. 'You're actin' kind of yellow of a sudden, Brant!'

Collier didn't like that and flushed, but he swallowed the insult, shaking his head. 'I've had nothing to do with all the rousting and sure not with those raids last night. I'm cutting out while I have a pretty clean slate.'

Dancey stared coldly. 'You agreed to everythin', but you never did like stickin' your neck out, did you? Case often said so, but like a damn fool, I stuck up for you! Ailin' health, I said, gettin' on in years, married daughter in Philadelphia, couple of grandkids. We settled just for lettin' you put in a little brainwork when we needed it and some cash — and by God we had to fight to get you to do that at times!'

'I-I'm settled now. I like this valley.

Might not like the sodbusters moving in but, if I have to, I can get by with what range I've got. It'll make a decent legacy to leave the grandkids. I guess I can live with the nesters havin' a little at the north end if I have to.'

'You blamed fool! How long you think they'll stay in that north section? Word gets out a dozen have settled in and next thing there'll be a hundred — all wantin' land from our range, pushin' us back into a corner where you can't swing a cat! Aaah, to hell with you, Brant! You wanna quit that's fine with me. I'll work somethin' out with Case! But before I go and before you finally decide: think on this — Durango's in jail. And Arlo's in charge while that fool Link goes and braces Nebraska!' He grinned crookedly. 'Reckon we won't see him again! Things're comin' together all of a sudden — you sure you wanna drop out right now, yellerbelly?'

He wrenched his horse's head around

and spurred away. Collier watched him go, feeling his stomach jump. *Dancey just could be right about a flood of homesteaders moving in . . . and with Durango locked up where he couldn't hurt no one . . .* Hell! He had some serious thinking to do!

* * *

Della was concerned about Durango. He had been unconscious when Link Waterman brought him down from O'Hagen's and the cut on his scalp from the gun barrel was deep.

She decided to ride into town, leaving Waco in charge. Salty had looked at her and nodded gently, still ashamed that he had allowed the remuda to be stolen.

'I'll make it up to you, ma'am,' he said quietly, moving from one foot to the other. 'I surely will.'

'Just do your job properly from now on, Salty.'

She rode out fast for town and did

not see that Waco and Salty had a few harsh words.

It was brief: Waco said they ought to get on with the general chores. Salty said, 'No, I meant what I said. I'll make things up to that gal . . . I'm gonna keep an eye on Nebraska and Case. A blind man can tell they're behind it.'

'Listen, Salt, you do what I say! She left me in charge!'

'Then you're in charge of yourself!' Salty growled, and stalked determinedly towards his already saddled mount.

* * *

Arlo Jeffries had enjoyed being a deputy before, even under Waterman. But the sheriff had fired him, not for any breach in his work — he was happy enough with that — but because Link figured to stretch his small budget, handle all the chores himself. Actually, it worked out well enough, for Arlo walked straight into the foreman's job with Dancey, but he still liked law-enforcement work better. *A little authority, seeing people jump when he spoke — well, it felt kind of good*.

He took his oath seriously when Link swore him in and that meant he ought to show concern for his prisoner's health. So he sent for Doc Mayfield and the medic was just leaving when Della arrived. She had a few brief words with him before going inside. But Deputy Jeffries wouldn't open the cell so Della could speak with Durango who was lying on the bunk, smoking and staring up at the adobe ceiling. He turned his head slowly when she spoke his name through the bars. She saw the white of a plaster strip where the doctor had stitched the scalp.

'How're you feeling, Durango?'

He smiled crookedly. 'About as strong as a newborn baby — I sound to myself like I'm talking into an empty barrel. I see things and hear things, but I don't seem to be in the same room as them . . . more standing in the doorway.'

'You still have a little concussion, Doc Mayfield says, you need to take it easy.'

'No trouble in doing that! Waterman swings a mean gun-butt — where is he by the way?'

'He's gone to see Nebraska.'

Durango's face straightened and he struggled to a sitting position, resting his wide shoulders against the wall. He let the room settle down from its sudden gyrations then looked at the girl. 'Nebraska'll kill him!'

'I think Link knows the risk, but he seems determined. Like he has something to prove.'

'Yeah. I've got to get outa here, Della!'

'Don't be foolish! What could you do anyway? Link will already be at Case's place.'

Durango smothered a quiet curse and settled back, slumping, nodding very gently. 'Then he's already a dead man.'

* * *

The entire crew at Case's ranch lied and backed up Nebraska's claim that he hadn't left his bunk at the J Bar C last night.

'Is that so?' said Waterman and there was a cocky, confident twist to his mouth that made Nebraska frown and Case himself lift a hand and rub his jaw gently.

The sheriff reached into his saddle-bag — noted how the movement made Nebraska tense — and pulled out a length of twine with a knot in it. He dismounted without a word, walked across to the big ramrod's horse, a dappled grey, and measured the string against the stirrup strap.

The knot reached to the bootplate of the stirrup iron and Link smiled wryly as he glanced up.

'Well, now, ain't that a coincidence! Your stirrups are set exactly to the same length as the ones on the saddle left on Durango's dead buckskin out at O'Hagen's.'

'Don't be loco,' Case said, before he

could stop himself. 'Durango ain't anywhere near as big as Nebraska . . .' As he realized that he was only confirming the sheriff's suspicions, he let his words trail off.

'You're right, Jace. Durango pointed that out to me when we found the dead hoss. So I took a measurement.' His gaze settled on Nebraska as he wound the twine around his fingers, but suddenly dropped his right hand and whipped out his Colt on that side of the buscadero rig, taking them all unawares. 'So, how about you come on in with me to the law office, Nebraska? An' we'll talk some more about this.'

The huge ramrod stiffened and his bad eyes narrowed dangerously. 'No one calls me a liar!'

'I ain't — yet. But we'll decide that when we get to the jailhouse.'

Nebraska spat. 'It'll be a cold day in Hell when you lock me up, Link!'

'Bring your bedroll then, 'cause that's where you're goin'.' He jerked the gun barrel. 'Now shuck that Colt!' He flicked his gaze to Case and the tensed cowboys. 'Jace, you stay outa this. Lotta folk know I'm here. Somethin' happens to me and you'll have a federal marshal showin' up on your doorstoop one mornin' right soon with a 'Please explain'. You want to push this that far?'

Case took his time shifting his gaze to his tight-lipped ramrod. 'Well, you better go along and sort this out, Nebraska,' the rancher said quietly, watched Nebraska stiffen and frown. 'I mean, we don't want any trouble *here on J Bar C*. I always try to keep trouble away from my own door, you know that.'

Waterman frowned, sensing there was something passing between the rancher and the giant, but not able to figure out just what.

Nebraska finally looked at the sheriff, eased his gun out and dropped it on the ground. 'All right. I'll go in with you but it won't change nothin'. Durango's got you horn-swoggled but I'm willin' to talk it out and convince you I had nothin' to do with them raids. But I ain't wearin' manacles! You try to put them on me, Link, an' I'll throw you over the goddamn bunkhouse!'

Link knew better than to push it and nodded. 'OK, but any fancy moves and I'll shoot you outa the saddle.'

Scowling, Nebraska moved towards his mount and spoke to one of the ranch hands. 'Shep, get my whipcord jacket off my bunk will you? Just in case Link here tosses me into one of his draughty old cells. The whipcord one now, not the canvas work jacket .. that's too tore-up.'

Shep, a flabby, shambling cowboy, nodded and went into the bunkhouse, coming back with Nebraska's stained brown jacket. The big foreman, mounted now, took it and shrugged into it, then nodded to the sheriff. 'Whenever you're ready.'

'Don't you keep him long, Link,' Case called. 'We got round-up in a few days.'

'You could be short-handed, Jace,' the sheriff said, and Case scowled as the sheriff fell in alongside Nebraska and they rode towards the trail to town.

* * *

Well clear of J Bar C, the trail dipped into a shallow basin choked with brush and Nebraska's grey edged off a little, got raked by some dry twigs. It began to snort and plunge: the sheriff didn't see Nebraska twisting one ear.

'The hell now!' demanded Waterman, bringing up the rifle he had resting across his thighs. 'You get that bronc settled down, Nebraska!'

'I'm .. doin' my . . . best, dammit!' the ramrod said, fighting the grey. During the confusion, his right hand dipped into the side pocket of the jacket and he brought out a small twin barrelled derringer. Waterman had ridden in closer to see for himself what was wrong with the grey and Nebraska's long arm reached out and rammed the derringer against Waterman's neck as he dropped the hammer.

The sheriff went sideways out of the saddle, blood spurting and splashing. His mount shied away and by that time Nebraska was out of the saddle, ran forward and fired the second barrel into Waterman's chest.

The lawman died instantly.

Curling a lip, Nebraska kicked the dead man brutally and spat on him, pocketing the derringer. He reached for his sixgun which he had seen the sheriff stuff into the saddle-bag.

Then a voice behind him said, 'Just hold it there you murderin' son of a bitch.'

Nebraska, hand still in the saddle-bag, snapped his head around. His thick eyebrows shot up as he recognized Salty. 'The hell you doin' here, you drunken bum?'

'I seen what you done and I'm takin' you in . . . '

That was as far as Salty got.

Nebraska fired through the flap of

the saddle-bag and the grizzled cow-hand jerked with the strike of lead. He triggered but his shot drove into the ground. Nebraska, smoking Colt free of the saddle-bag now, fired three more times, blowing Salty out of the saddle, the scrawny body jerking with the impact of each bullet.

Nebraska reloaded, looking at the two men he had just killed.

'Well, Jace, just what you wanted — I never let it happen on J Bar C land!'

12

'HANG THE SCUM!'

Della was reluctant to leave town with Durango still in jail. There was no need for it and she wondered just how she was going to convince Link Waterman of that.

He was stubborn and stupid in many ways, but she felt he was only trying to do what he saw as his job. Arlo was unapproachable, puffed-up with his own sudden importance. She saw Big John Dancey in town with some of his men and she felt uneasy, though she couldn't put a name to the exact cause. *Something was brewing here* . . .

But she decided she had better get on back to the spread and see how Salty and Waco were doing. It was when she was riding out of the livery that she saw Waco heading into town fast, eyes scanning folk on the board-walks, finally heading towards the law office. She knew he was searching for her and that uneasy feeling increased as she rode her horse into full view and waved, eventually catching Waco's eye.

The man spun his mount, some folk staring at his speed, as he skidded to a halt. Della's hands tightened on her reins as she saw his face. 'What's wrong, Waco?'

He wiped sweat from his eyebrows. 'Salty went to keep an eye on Nebraska — I couldn't stop him! He said he had to make up for lettin' the remuda get stole and — '

Very tense now, her breathing coming in short gasps, she said, 'What happened!'

'Well, I started to get worried as the day wore on and he never come back so I rode out towards J Bar C . . . '

* * *

Waco didn't want to go near that ranch. He was no coward, but he knew the hardcases who worked for Jason Case, had run into them on more than one occasion in Two Rivers. He didn't want trouble, but he had to know if Salty was OK. They had been pards for a long time.

He decided to cut around and approach from the town end in case someone was watching for riders from Della's.

That was when he found Nebraska with two dead men roped over their mounts. It took him only a moment to identify Salty and Sheriff Link Waterman.

* * *

Della stared at Waco's announcement. 'Are you telling me the sheriff and Salty are both dead?'

Waco nodded. 'Yeah. I got some Sioux in me, ma'am, and I can read tracks real good. I let Nebraska get outa sight then went down to where I'd seen some dark stains — they were blood-stains, made by someone who'd took a fall from a hoss. It was Waterman's hoss's tracks, and I found Nebraska's where he'd rid in real close, maybe to get a better shot.'

'You think Nebraska killed Link? *Murdered him*?'

'That's the way the sign reads, ma'am. The other blood was some yards off where a rider'd come crashin' outa the brush. The tracks were from Salty's hoss — and he musta been shot up pretty bad. There was a whole slew of blood.'

'Nebraska again?'

'Has to be. Both blood patches were still damp.'

Della was shaking a little now as the news sank in. 'Where was Nebraska going?'

'Towards town here. I took the Half Moon cut-off.' He turned and looked towards the bridge. 'He'll be arrivin' soon, before sundown, I reckon. I din' know what to do so I come lookin' for you.'

'You did right, Waco. I-I'm just trying

to figure out why Nebraska would bring men he's murdered into town . . .'

'Well, here he comes!'

They heard the clip-clop of hoofs on the planks of the arched wooden bridge and saw Nebraska riding in slowly through the afternoon light, made gloomy by gathering clouds, leading the two horses with dead men roped across their backs. Already a crowd was gathering, questioning Nebraska, some men running on into town and spreading the news excitedly. 'The sheriff's dead!'

'Looks like that rummy done it, one they call Salty!'

Those words stirred Della and she spurred her mount towards the law office where Nebraska was obviously heading, calling over her shoulder, 'Bring Doc Mayfield, Waco!'

Waco wondered why a sawbones would be needed for men already dead, but he did as he was told and when he got back a small crowd had formed outside the law office.

Arlo Jeffries was standing on the landing, looking down at the dead men now laid out at his feet. He stared hard at Nebraska. 'You say you seen what happened?'

'Yeah, more or less.'

'You did, or you didn't! Which is it?'

'I heard the shootin' and by the time I got there, Link was down on one knee, blood everywhere, shootin' his rifle fast as he could work the lever — at Salty. Knocked him clean off his feet. Hit him dead square, three, four times.'

'Salty wouldn't shoot the sheriff!' protested Waco angrily, and Nebraska shrugged his big shoulders.

'Tellin' you what I seen — and I seen Link was dead, half his throat shot out. Salty was bad hit but still alive. I kinda persuaded him a little to tell me what in hell he thought he was doin', killin' the sheriff like that . . . '

Nebraska paused and looked around at the crowd, smiling crookedly. They knew what he meant by 'persuaded'.

'You son of a bitch!' Waco murmured but made no move towards the big man. Nebraska smiled crookedly.

'Salty said Durango told him if he was locked up it meant Link must've worked out who pulled that raid on the homesteaders. Only way to get outa the trouble was to kill Link — and Salty done what he was told.'

Waco swore, barely able to contain himself. There was an angry murmur from the crowd and Della stepped forward. 'Has anyone ever called you a liar to your face, Nebraska?' she snapped.

His eyes narrowed. 'Not and walked away more'n two steps,' he said in his deep rumbling voice.

'Well, I'm doing it! You're a downright liar!'

The crowd was suddenly silent. Nebraska pursed his lips, glanced around at Arlo and then turned to Della. 'Seein' as you're a woman, that makes you lucky, but I wouldn't push it.' Before she could reply he turned back to Arlo. 'It's gospel, Arlo. That Salty'd do anythin' for a free drink, everyone knows that. And he sure reeks of booze. See for yourself.'

Arlo gestured to Mayfield who was examining the bodies. 'Doc?'

'I smell whiskey all right.' Mayfield lowered his grey head towards Salty's sagging jaw, sniffed, looked up quickly. 'Bad teeth is all I smell in his mouth — but his clothes are splashed with whiskey. Almost as much as there is blood!'

'Salty never had no redeye when he left the spread,' spoke up Waco, but Nebraska merely shrugged, smiling faintly as if to say 'Prove it, 'breed!'

'Someone musta give him some — likely that gunslinger when he told him to shoot the sheriff. Bribed him.' Nebraska planted that thought firmly with the crowd, looking around with his hard eyes. 'Hell, I never had much use for Waterman, like most of you, he was a damn nuisance most times, but he tried to do his job. An' he did make this town safe for women and kids to walk the streets any time of day or night. He sure din' deserve to be murdered in cold blood.'

That stirred the townsfolk because they saw their safe town as Link Waterman's one and only positive accomplishment during his time in office. It counted a lot with family men who had to live with Saturday nights given over to drunken, brawling cow-hands ranging the streets in search of trouble — until Waterman got an ordinance passed that required any man entering town on a Saturday to check his guns at the law office before he went about his business — or pleasure. It worked, because at that time the big three had wanted to be seen as co-operative good citizens, so they ordered their men to comply.

'Now the sheriff's dead,' Nebraska continued, 'and unless Arlo Jeffries shows a lot more spunk than he has in the past, this town is gonna go to hell in a handbasket . . . '

No one believed that Nebraska felt anything but contempt for Link and the town ordinance, but if what he was saying was true . . . cold-blooded murder could not be condoned, whoever was accused of it.

Big John Dancey came pushing through, some of his men beside him. He looked steadily at Nebraska as he spoke up.

'Yeah, Link did what he could, dumb as he was, but he showed he could stick to his guns when he had to. Hell, he made sure that gunslinger was locked up till he looked into them raids last night — and even from the jailhouse, that son of a bitch reached out and closed Link's mouth for good!'

Dancey looked around at the crowd: they were listening to him because over the years they had gotten used to doing just that, even if it was mostly because of being bullied into it. Della saw which way things were going and so did the doctor. 'You'd best come away, Della. It's going to get mighty ugly around here.'

She shook off his arm. 'But don't you see what's going on? The alliance arranged Link's murder and now Nebraska is trying to blame it on Durango!'

'And Salty!' growled Waco, angry but knowing his limitations. He knew he could never face-down Nebraska.

'Unfortunately, my dear,' the doctor said to Della, 'Dancey seems to have the crowd's ear.' He added quietly, 'By the way, Salty's wounds were not caused by a rifle — they're from a handgun. I've seen a lot of gunshot wounds and I'll stake my reputation on it. Dancey has men scattered amongst this crowd. It could develop into a very dangerous situation, Della.'

She felt sick as she heard the roar from the crowd.

Someone yelled, '*That damn gunslinger seems to figure he can do what he likes*!' One of Dancey's crew, of course.

'*Not while he's locked up he cain't — I say we make sure he stays that way*!'

'*Better still — hang the scum!*'

Della recognized that voice as belonging to Pete Delaney, Dancey's wrangler: planting Dancey's notions in the receptive minds of the uneasy and somewhat bewildered townsfolk.

'*Get outa the way, Arlo, we're comin' to get him!*' someone else called.

'No you ain't!' Arlo had quietly stepped back inside the office and now reappeared holding a scattergun, menacing the stirring crowd, both hammers cocked. 'You're gonna clear the streets and keep 'em cleared! I'm the law here now! Go on home before I start spillin' a little blood myself.'

Dancey glowered. 'Who said you're the law?'

'I did! I took an oath when Link made me deputy and part of that oath says if anythin' happens to the sheriff, the deputy takes over!'

'Until such time as he's relieved,' Dancey snapped. 'I figure you're relieved, Arlo. Just don't expect your old job back, pullin' a deal like this!'

'You can't relieve me, Big John: it can only be done by election, or by another duly sworn representative of United States law of higher office.'

Dancey frowned, his mouth like a steel trap. 'I din' even know you could read more'n your own name and a cattle tally! You been studyin' up, you son of a bitch, ain't you?'

Arlo nodded, very serious. 'I have. I've always liked bein' a lawman but you made me an offer before I couldn't refuse after Link decided not to use a deputy. Workin' for you, I've seen both sides of the Law, Big John — *Ah-ha*! You don't like me bringin' that subject up, eh? Okay. I'll leave it sit for now, because of old times. But you think about me workin' for you, what I did for you, what I know . . . '

'I'll be rememberin', Arlo!' Dancey gritted. 'OK, play the sheriff!' Dancey looked around at the mob. 'But I think I'll take these men here down to the saloon and buy 'em all some drinks while we talk things over. They just might not want you for a lawman!'

There was a ragged cheer from the mob and they started to move away up the street towards the nearest saloon. Dancey gave Della a smirking smile as he followed.

Her grip tightened on Doc Mayfield's arm. 'Can't you see what he's doing? He's going to keep the liquor flowing, work them up into a lynch mob!'

'I'm afraid I have to agree, Della. This has turned even more ugly than I figured.' He removed her hand from his arm. 'I have to get back to the infirmary, make it secure, and get bandages and lotions ready.'

'Is — is that all you're going to do?'

The medic paused and gave her a helpless look. 'I'm sixty-one years old, Della. I have a wife and a daughter who is bound to a wheelchair for the rest of her life. What would you have me do? I'm not like your gunslinger friend — he's the one's caused all this, scaring decent folk lily-livered, wondering who he came to kill. You made a big mistake bringing him in here, Della. I'm sorry, but that's the way I see it.'

She started to protest that she hadn't sent for Durango but the doctor hurried off and she watched him go, then turned towards the law office. Arlo had already given his permission for the impatient undertaker to remove the dead men and had closed the office doors. Even as she started forward she heard the bar drop across on the inside.

'Waco, we've got to do something! Arlo can't hold off a lynch mob!'

'Me an' Arlo always got along pretty good. Mebbe I can have a word with him.' Waco stepped up on to the boardwalk and rapped his knuckles on the law-office door.

'Arlo? It's Waco — Miz Shaw'd like to talk with you. You know you can trust her. An' me — we've bought each other drinks on a Sat'd'y night . . . '

There was a long silence and then Waco rapped again. 'C'mon, Arlo! Can't you hear 'em in the saloon? They're already raisin' hell, and Dancey and Nebraska're whippin' up a mob! There ain't a lot of time, *amigo*! An', you ask me, you can do with all the help you can get!'

Della waited and then relaxed as she heard the door bar being removed.

At the same time, the first heavy drops of rain spattered down and there was a ripping sound as lightning zigzagged over the surrounding hills.

The law-office door opened about a foot and she glimpsed Arlo's white face, and the gleam of the lightning flash on the muzzles of the scattergun still held in his hands.

'You better come in before you get wet.'

His voice sounded remarkably calm and, as Della stepped through the door, she wondered if he had already worked out some sort of plan.

She hoped so, because she was stymied.

And more than a little afraid as she heard another roar from the mob boozing it up in the saloon.

13

RIOT

It was hard to see clearly in the noisy bar room because of the thick haze of tobacco smoke. It was also hard to hear because of the deafening rain on the roof and other buildings close by, plus the shouting and yelling as the drinks flowed endlessly and men became drunker, more boisterous. Decent folk were safely locked up behind doors.

Nebraska's eyes were becoming red and bleak because of the drinking and his own mood. 'Black Hills hell! Me an' Case go way back.' He snorted. 'The things we done . . . '

'He must pay well — though I hear he's strugglin' even more'n me since that last trail went wrong for us.'

Nebraska's words were a little slurred

and he sounded suspicious. 'Don't you worry none about Case. He's OK for cash now.'

'After the raids, you mean?'

Nebraska's mean eyes slitted. 'Is that what I mean?'

'Thought it was.' Dancey figured he had better not give away how much he'd figured out. You could never tell which way this son of a bitch was going to jump. They had put away a lot of booze together over the years and it was always the same: watch Nebraska for signs of hostility — then watch yourself! But work him right and he could be a good source of information. 'Seein' as O'Hagen's outa things now,' Dancey added, trying to sound casual.

'What the hell's O'Hagen got to do with it?'

Dancey shrugged. 'He was last of the nesters near J Bar C, wasn't he? Now he's dead an' his place is empty.'

Nebraska turned side on to the bar so he was squarely facing Dancey. 'You might be buyin' the drinks, Big John, but you're gettin' to be a pain in the ass.'

'Then stop drinkin' my likker.'

Nebraska straightened. 'You crowdin' me?'

Dancey smiled crookedly. 'Hell, no. Just wanted to get your attention, let you know I'm with you.'

'With me? In what?'

'Makin' a lynch mob outa this bunch of dummies, help you square things with Durango. That's what you want, ain't it? You an' Case both owe him from Dakota, but Case's lyin' low, ain't he? You're the one on show if anythin' goes wrong.'

Nebraska scrubbed a hand over his jaw, stubble rasping. His eyes seemed redder than ever and maybe he swayed slightly. 'Case'll thank me later for them raids. He just needed a little nudge to get him goin': was gettin' too settled, waitin' things out, steada doin'.'

Dancey smiled. 'Waitin' for them sod-busters to throw in their hands?' Dancey snorted. 'Till hell freezes!

Durango's backin' 'em and he's the one we gotta get rid of — once he's gone, the rest'll run after last night. You gave Case what he wanted — got rid of that crazy Irishman . . . Time to get on with the rest of it now.'

Nebraska towered above Dancey, crowding him. 'Big John, you are pushin' yourself right into more trouble than you can shake a stick at.'

Dancey held up a hand and hoped it didn't tremble — time to be mighty leery of Nebraska in this kind of mood. There was a loco streak in him, a liking for killing and maiming — and he'd seen the big ramrod in action enough times to make him wary. Have to throw a hitch on what I'm saying, he told himself silently. Come at it from another angle.

'Nebraska, I told you: I'm with you all the way. Just cut me in an' you won't be alone.'

'I work best alone.' He was getting pretty drunk now.

'Most times I feel the same way, but

sometimes a little co-operation is best.' Nebraska, swaying, didn't look convinced. 'So, we get these drunken fools in the mood for lynchin', right? Move down to the jailhouse and get it done, and if Arlo gets caught up in things . . . ' He shrugged. 'Well, I can tell he's gonna be a gut-ache if somethin' ain't done about him, too.'

'Never did like Arlo. When he was Link's deputy before, he come at me with a scattergun once an' I had to back down. Case wouldn't let me touch him after he went to work for you. But I don't forget them things.'

Dancey grinned, spread his hands. 'Be my guest . . . Arlo don't count with me any longer. Always bitchin' about somethin'. There's that gal, too . . . She needs taken care of.'

Nebraska nodded, his eyes like coffin nails as he said, 'The bitch called me a liar in front of half the town.'

Big John Dancey nodded soberly: that was good enough for him. Just the kind of thing Nebraska could handle.

* * *

Durango had a mighty sore head, his temples throbbing, his ears ringing. But not so badly that he couldn't hear the commotion coming from the saloon.

He recognized it for what it was: a big mob boozing it up and, as he couldn't think of any likely cause for common celebration, he reckoned maybe someone was buying the drinks. Someone having a birthday, maybe . . .

Or deliberately working up a riot.

He didn't want to think any further than that but he knew with someone like Nebraska, backed by Jason Case, and likely Dancey and Collier, as well — he had the gut-feeling things weren't looking the brightest. For him.

Then he heard people coming into the passage and he stood up, a little dizzy, steadying on the wall before he went to the barred door. He was surprised to see Della and Waco, with Arlo a few paces behind, carrying his sawn-off shotgun, sheriff's star shiny on his vest.

Della came right up to the bars, touched one of his hands where they gripped the iron. 'You've probably heard the racket coming from the saloon, Durango. I'm afraid Dancey and Nebraska are doing their best to work up a lynch mob.'

The gunfighter flicked his gaze past Waco to Arlo.

'You gonna gimme a chance, deputy?'

'Sheriff, now.' Arlo had told him earlier about Link and Salty and Nebraska's story — and made it clear that he wasn't about to swallow it. But he seemed an unrelenting kind of *hombre* and Durango wondered if Arlo would be fool enough to try to hold off a rioting lynch mob alone.

'Question still stands — Sheriff.'

'Della here and Waco have sorta convinced me you been set-up, but fact remains it was Link who slugged you, so that means he had some reason to do it. Mebbe just until he checked things out, but there's a lot here that don't set easy with me.'

'Oh, come on, Arlo!' broke in Della impatiently. 'Don't beat around the bush! You agreed in your office only minutes ago to give Durango a chance! Listen to the mob! We can't delay!'

Arlo was very serious, his gaze touching each of them, settling on Durango. 'I dunno if I'm doin' the right thing. I've heard you keep your word and I know Della can be trusted, so I'm gonna let you go in her custody. You run out and she's the one in trouble, you savvy?'

Durango nodded but he was looking at the girl. 'You're sticking your neck out for me — again. Like you did when you swore to Link I'd spent the night with you — which I hadn't — but whether it was true or not you've lost a deal of standing in this valley.'

She waved it aside, turned to the sheriff. 'Come on, Arlo! Don't fuss! Get the door open!'

'Crowd's bustin' outa the saloon,'

Waco said and they all heard the new, louder sounds as the shouts reached them through the hammering rain.

Arlo had beads of sweat on his face now, and, somewhat reluctantly, he set down the shotgun and took the keys from his belt. Durango got his hat from the bunk and was standing in the passage a minute later.

'I need my guns, Arlo.'

Jeffries pursed his lips, hesitated, then nodded. 'I guess — but you remember what I said about bringing trouble down on Della.'

'*Arlo*! Will you *please* hurry up!' pleaded the girl.

In the front office, the lawman unlocked a cupboard, reluctantly handed Durango his sixgun and bullet belt and then his rifle. 'You finished with Dancey now?' Durango asked.

Arlo hesitated, nodded. 'He paid well and I — I let the money compromise me for a while, I guess. Dancey figures Case's got some stolen gold stashed away someplace and he aims to get his share. That's all he's interested in. Double-crossin' someone who's s'posed to be his pard!' He shook his head, unable to stomach such treachery.

'No honour among thieves, Arlo.'

The sheriff nodded, wary now Durango was wearing his guns. 'You stay with Della. You might have to run but she'll be with you — I want you back here by sundown tomorrow.' The shotgun lifted and covered Durango. 'I'll decide then just what I'm gonna do with you . . . '

Durango nodded. 'You've got my word — and thanks.'

Waco had already gone out the rear door and Della said anxiously, 'They'll send someone to cover the back . . . '

Durango took her arm, carrying his rifle in his other hand and moved swiftly towards the rear door.

From the front, they could already hear slurred voices yelling for Arlo to open the door before they kicked it in.

'An' bring out that murderin' gunhawk!' someone added. 'We got a mighty strong rope here just the size of his neck!'

Arlo cursed and hurried back down the passage. Once in his office he locked the cellblock door and went to the barred street door, looking through the rain-streaked window beside it. The water distorted his view but he saw a solid phalanx of shouting, gesturing men out there — and then came sudden gunfire from the rear of the jailhouse.

A ragged volley of shots.

* * *

Waco had their horses ready and waiting, himself sitting his saddle and looking anxious as Della and Durango came running towards him from the back of the jailhouse, the gunfighter moving a mite slow.

Della went to her chestnut, Durango to the claybank Waco had brought for him. Mounted, they were turning towards the brush beyond the rubbish and tangled weeds when there was a shout. 'They're gettin' away!'

The words were swiftly followed by gunfire, several men appearing, a couple in slickers, others just in their ordinary clothes, drenched by the downpour. The heavy rain threw their aim, too, and their bullets were wild.

Della crouched low and Durango gestured curtly to Waco to get her away as he palmed up his sixgun. His shots blasted hard on the tail of those fired by the mob and his stunning speed of return fire stopped them in their tracks.

Lead splashed into the mud at their feet, a bullet ricocheted from the jail building. The men scattered, stumbling and falling over each other in their hurry to get away.

But there was a crush of more rioters running down the side alley, yelling, shooting wildly, forcing the retreating men back towards the rear of the building. They resisted, yelling that Durango was out and doing the shooting. It became a struggling mêlée that blocked that part of the narrow alley.

'Get clear! Get clear, dammit!' roared Nebraska in his rumbling voice, slashing with his Colt. 'Judas priest!'

Dancey was shouting, too, seeing the trio disappearing on horseback into the brush. Frustratedly, he emptied his gun after them and then a small bunch of riders skidded into view, coming out of the next alley along. He recognized Case in the lead and knew someone had gotten word to him about the happenings in town.

'Nebraska! There's Case! Forget this drunken mob! Find some mounts! We'll handle this ourselves.'

Nebraska had already turned and began throwing men aside as if they were sacks of straw, clearing a path back up the alley. The drunks staggered out of the way, some looking about bewilderedly, wondering what the hell they were doing here with all the guns going off around them.

Then, as Dancey and Nebraska broke

through and ran for the street, Arlo Jeffries appeared with his shotgun. He fired over their heads, cocking the second hammer instantly.

Dancey was a heartbeat behind Nebraska as they dived into the mud. Arlo's scattergun blasted again. Buckshot whistled above them and Dancey instinctively covered his head with his arms, but Nebraska rolled on to his side and triggered his Colt: two fast shots. Arlo staggered, hit once, swinging away from the big ramrod. The sheriff lurched back around the corner as he realized the gun was empty, but Nebraska was up, dripping mud, lunging after him. Arlo was fumbling to reload as Nebraska rounded the corner of the law building and skidded to a stop, broken teeth bared in a tight grin. Arlo was down on one knee, blood on his shirt, spreading pinkly in the rain, his hands slipping on the wet steel of the still unloaded scattergun. Gamely, he reached for his Colt and Nebraska coldly shot him in the back. The lawman crashed full length as Dancey came up, blowing out his cheeks.

'Looks like this town needs a new sheriff,' Nebraska grinned happily, starting to move away, reloading as he went. 'Might even apply for the job — after I nail that son of a bitch Durango!'

They sprinted for the hitch rail where mounts were tethered, half-blinded by the driving rain storm. Thunder crashed overhead, hard on the heels of a jagged streak of lightning. *A night fit for neither man nor beast to be out.*

But ideal for a killing.

14

STAND AND FIGHT

Most of the townsmen gave up early. The rain pounded down, flattened the floppy brims of some hats, stung through rents in slickers, caused one or two of the mounts to shy as the drops pelted their hides. Small hail raked the riders like buckshot and gradually the posse dwindled, the booze-induced enthusiasm fast wearing off as several defected.

The rest, sobering very fast now, wondered why the hell they were here? They didn't have to be. They were volunteers, had a choice. And hot food and a fire in the grate was mighty attractive. So, by the time the posse had reached the hills, there were barely a dozen riders, consisting mostly of cowhands from the Big

Three's ranches. They had no chance of finding tracks in this. But a good chance of riding into an ambush, some griped to Nebraska.

'If you can't see your hand in front of your face, Durango sure ain't gonna see well enough to bushwhack you!' snarled the ramrod. But the men weren't convinced and their hearts weren't in the search, anyway, by this time.

'Call it off till the rain eases,' suggested Shep from Case's spread. 'They'll go to ground.'

'They will if they got more sense than us,' allowed one of the few remaining townsmen. The posse agreed sullenly.

Dancey wiped a hand down his muddy, streaming face. 'You stick!' he ordered. 'This is the best chance we've had of gettin' Durango — no one else leaves!'

There were murmurings as he glared around through the wall of gusting rain. Nebraska and Case backed Big John, and no one defected, but the urge to do so was still there.

The posse spread out and began a wide sweep of the hills, muddy rivulets splashing down on them. Slowly, a few dropped back, eventually managed to slip away and disappear. The others could hear a roaring in the distance: both rivers were rising rapidly. *Yet another worry . . .*

* * *

'I've never seen it like this before,' Della said, having to shout even in the shallow cave where the three of them were taking shelter from the hammering rain.

'I was down on the Red one time and the river broke its banks . . . was like an inland sea for weeks, mud up to your armpits long after that,' Waco told the others.

'I saw the Mississippi run a banker once,' Durango said, watching outside through the veil of water even as he spoke. 'But it wasn't raining as hard as this — seems more like a cloudburst than a storm.'

Della, shivering, face wet and pinched, nodded worriedly. 'Our homestead land mostly lies in between the two rivers. I'm on more of a rise than the others, but my cattle could still be in danger if the rivers flood.'

'Nothing we can do, Della,' the gunfighter told her gently. 'When it eases, you and Waco should head back — I can handle this OK. More in my line than yours, anyway.'

'We — we'll see,' she said, and he could tell she was distracted by concern for the safety of her spread. He didn't like being here in the cave, preferred open space around him, plenty of escape routes for the choosing.

They would do their best to kill him this time, he knew that. For the posse, it was even better that he had gotten out before the lynch party arrived. Now the whole deal could be set-up to look like nothing more than the hunting down of an escaped prisoner who chose to stand and fight.

Because that's what he aimed to do.

Now was the time to finish this. All the way . . .

Waco heard them first. He was closest to the mouth of the cave, fully alert, and he wanted to avenge his pard: he felt obliged to make up in some way for Salty letting down Durango and Della with his failure to watch the ranch the night the remuda was stolen. Salty had already paid the full price, but Waco figured they had been pards long enough for him to do something on Salty's behalf: *avenge him* — he didn't give a thought to the possible consequences to himself.

A vague sound reached him. Eyes squinted, he strained to see and — *there!* — just a faint smudge between the trees where the timber thinned. A horseman, and another to one side.

'They're here,' Waco called softly into the cave, and he heard the instant stirring beside him. Durango was crouched there, rifle in hand.

It took the gunfighter a few moments

to make out the approaching riders through the rain. They were having trouble on the muddy slope, horses slipping, men fighting the reins.

'Too interested in getting up the slope to notice the cave yet,' the gunfighter opined. 'Only a matter of time, though. They likely won't see us at first, but they'll make for it for shelter if they got any sense.'

Durango jerked his head for Waco to follow him back to where Della stood, huddled in her slicker, feeling the cold.

'Waco, you take Della, slip out the left-hand side of the entrance . . . just listen, damnit, there's no time to argue! You get Della back to her spread, and stay there with her.'

'While you do what?' Waco demanded.

'Lead 'em away in the opposite direction.'

'Hell, you dunno these hills! In this rain you'll be lost in five minutes, likely ride right into 'em!'

'If I do, you'll hear the gunfire. But keep riding.'

Della quickly put a hand on his arm. 'Durango, you can't do it! Waco's right: you don't know this country.'

'I can handle whoever's out there. I'm not making out I'm a one-man army, but if I can't hold off that bunch I deserve all I get.' He suddenly grabbed her, lifted her bodily onto her horse. She had to duck instinctively as the roof sloped down here. He forced the reins into her numbed hands. 'Waco, go with her. Now! She won't stand a chance alone.'

'I ain't sure you will, either,' Waco allowed but he mounted his horse carefully. He was reluctant to go but he knew Durango was right: the girl had to have protection. 'I hope I see you again, Durango.'

'You will.' But the gunfighter wasn't feeling as confident as he tried to sound. He slapped his wet hat across the rump of Waco's horse and, an instant later, Della's mount. As they cleared the entrance, Durango ran forward and threw himself down on the right-hand side of the entrance, several yards away. He could just make out the first of the riders below now as he brought his rifle to his shoulder.

Before the men could spot Della and Waco fleeing from the left, Durango started shooting, raking the ragged line below. Most of his lead showered down wet leaves and twigs but one shot knocked a horse sideways, the rider cursing as he threw himself from the saddle. He began to slide, yelling loudly as his wounded mount slid down behind him — and overtook him within a few yards. The screaming stopped abruptly. The horse kept on sliding past the broken, still body: it was Shep from Case's spread.

The others scattered and hunted cover, fighting mounts frightened by the suddenness of the attack.

'Hunt cover!' That was Nebraska's bellowing voice. The big man wrenched his mount's head down, but corrected quickly as the forefeet began to slide. He was still fighting for control when one of Durango's shots burned across his beefy shoulders. He tumbled out of the saddle, lost his grip on the wet, slippery reins and found himself sliding with the muddy run-off. Instinct made him grab a tree root exposed by the heavy rain and he hauled himself in behind the trunk, panting. He fumbled frantically to get his sixgun out of the holster under his sodden jacket. His rifle was still in the scabbard on his thrashing horse.

Durango emptied the Winchester, flattened himself against the rock where small cascades spurted, fumbling cartridges with cold wet fingers. He dropped a few but managed to fill the magazine. Then the first shots from below whined off the cave's entrance, showering him with mud and rock chips.

He rolled part way across the opening, his clothes sodden now, cold water making him shiver briefly. At least it had helped clear his still throbbing head. Settling behind a low barrier of rock, he ducked as a bullet screeched away only inches from his face. The gunflash below gave him a target and he fired slightly above and to the left.

A man's body was flung half upright and then backwards, skidding downslope. Durango didn't wait to see any more, shifted aim, triggered again and another man yelled and staggered up in a double-over position. He started to run, fell and slid. Durango's next shots splashed him with more mud and the last one punched through the already torn slicker. The man grunted, rolled more violently, bringing up against a tree base.

'Hell almighty! He's killin' us all!' a man yelled.

Durango saw someone jump up and literally hurl himself down the slope, not even attempting to run, just hitting the mud on his chest and sliding like a sled on snow. Before he was out of sight, two more men were following him, running, falling, sliding, righting themselves awkwardly.

The gunfighter deliberately fired high, hurrying them along. But there were still at least half a dozen left, likely the hardcases from the alliance. He glimpsed Nebraska as the man ducked out and back quickly behind his tree. Durango fired just for the hell of it, a white ragged strip tearing the bark. He smiled thinly. That would make the big man think twice about moving again.

Big John Dancey was easily recognizable, crouched by a sapling that didn't afford his large body full protection. But the man had a rifle and as Durango started to drop, the rancher fired and the gunfighter felt the jarring impact and searing pain of a bullet ripping into his left tricep.

It turned him part way round and knocked him flat. He tore off his wet neckerchief, reached in under his jacket and wadded the cloth over the wound. Warm blood coursed across his flesh and fingers as Dancey yelled,

'I got him! *I got the son of a bitch*!'

'You gonna go up an' make sure?'

asked Nebraska sounding sceptical.

'He got him all right.' That was Jason Case himself. 'I seen Durango drop.'

'We-ell — I'll cover you two while you go up and finish him off if he ain't already dead.' There was sarcasm in Nebraska's words.

He didn't get any reply from Dancey but Case said, 'You're a very funny man, Nebraska!'

Durango stayed low. If they thought he was hit bad he might as well take time to try and staunch the flow of blood from the wound. The fingers on his left hand were numbed now and there was hot pain flooding up his neck. He ripped the seam of his shirt, pushed down his jacket, exposing his bullet-torn shoulder. It hurt enough to make him grimace. But he managed to wrap the neckerchief around his arm and use his teeth to tie the knot directly over the wound, hoping the pressure would help stop the bleeding. He rearranged his clothing and must have shown a part of his body or maybe his hat, for two guns blasted and bullets screamed off the low rock barrier that sheltered him.

'He's still alive!' bawled Case, his heart hammering up into his throat with the knowledge. 'Goddammit! Why can't you shoot straighter, John!' Case was so incensed, he half lifted up to roar at Big John Dancey.

Durango fired the rifle one-handed, the fore-end resting in a natural groove in the rock. The gun jumped but he had pulled the butt in tightly against his right shoulder and still had some control over the weapon. Case slammed over, disappearing from sight.

'Judas!' Dancey said. 'Jace? Jace! You OK!' No answer. 'One of you cowboys go check him!'

'Check him yourself,' a ragged, nervous voice told him. 'I'm gettin' outa here!'

'You stay put or I'll shoot you!' Nebraska threatened but there was sudden movement slightly downslope from him as a man stood and hurled himself away from the approaches to the cave.

Nebraska swore, lifted his sixgun and triggered twice. The man somersaulted, the bullets striking him high in the shoulders, spinning him on an invisible fulcrum.

'That was helpful!' snapped Dancey.

'Sure. Now the others'll stay put.'

'What others?' Dancey asked bitterly. 'While we were watchin' that one you just shot, the other two vamoosed!'

A stunned silence now — except for the endless rain.

Then Nebraska called, 'How's Case?'

'Down — and that's all I want to know. I ain't goin' lookin' to see how bad he's hit!' Dancey broke off at a sudden noise. 'Nebraska! What the hell . . . *You son of a bitch! Come back here*!'

But the giant ramrod had made his move while Dancey was talking, knowing Durango's attention would be at least partly diverted by the rancher. Dancey moved now, crouching, running to a bigger tree for protection. Durango's lead chewed a handful of spraying bark from the trunk as the man skidded behind, breathless, still mentally cursing Nebraska. He could hear him down the slope, searching for one of the mounts — if there were any still around.

Dancey chose a careful line, keeping a thick-trunked tree between himself and the cave, and began to slide down on his backside, hitching himself along, staying as low as possible. Durango couldn't see him and moved to another position, left arm dangling at his side. The pain was increasing now and he had to stop, dizzy, and lean his good shoulder against part of the rock wall. Dancey and Nebraska could have made it safely off the mountain by this time. There was no sound from where Case had fallen and the other cowhands had quit, were a long way from here by now.

Slowly, painfully, he mounted the claybank Waco and Della had brought him, and slumped forward as he kicked in his heels. The animal walked out into the rain which showed no signs of abating. Durango forced himself to straighten, rifle at the ready. He would have to use it one-handed. If he was lying prone, he could manage a fairly accurate shot but not being able to grip the fore-end so he could control the recoil he would miss more times than he hit his target, trying to shoot from the saddle.

So he sheathed the wet Winchester and slid his Colt from his holster. The familiar feel of the smooth, worn butt gave him confidence as he searched for the missing men.

It was hard controlling the claybank and he was forced to holster the Colt so he could manipulate the reins. His left hand was almost useless now, numbed by the wound up his arm. Obviously there were damaged nerves. But he made a precarious way down, glimpsed a rider through a slight break in a squall of rain. The man was below him, almost down, but riding across the slope, his only interest, flight.

Then Durango squinted against the driving rain. The flats had become a lake! Spray fanned as Dancey spurred his mount into the muddy water, fetlock deep at first, climbing higher up the mount with each stride. The rivers had broken their banks . . .

Standing in the stirrups, Durango saw that the water spread out ahead and to both sides for as far as he could see. The land was inundated. Lying in between the rivers here, the flood churned across the flats from each watercourse, finally meeting in a muddy cauldron.

Killdeer Valley was fast becoming an inland sea. Some sections would be completely under water — he shook his head, rain flying from the sodden hat brim, trying to bring himself back to the present. And just in time —

Dancey had decided to make one last stand when he saw the flood ahead, knew it would slow down his escape. So he whirled his frightened mount now, defiantly galloping back towards the gunfighter, standing in the stirrups with rifle to his shoulder. Durango's right hand suddenly came up with flame stabbing from his Colt. Dancey's tall body jerked and twisted as he was smashed back onto his mount's rump, rolled off to splash into the churning water as the horse ran on.

Durango wrenched around as he felt the air-whip of lead cracking past his face: it was Nebraska, unmistakable, a giant centaur charging in with battered, twisted mouth, his rifle blazing. But his horse was running raggedly, because of the surging flood, and every shot was wild.

Durango, lying low on the claybank now, spurred on, looping the reins around his numbed left forearm, to keep the tension on the bit before the horse took it between its teeth. Nebraska desperately slanted the rifle, aiming for the racing claybank's chest.

Durango suddenly thrust upright in the saddle, the left arm jerking on the reins, bringing his mount's head up. It instinctively slowed in response to the sudden pressure. Nebraska missed but he wasn't about to give up. Durango took deliberate aim even as a bullet *zipped* overhead. He triggered twice and Nebraska shuddered, sagged right. His rifle fell and the horse slowed uncertainly. Durango rode in warily, hammer cocked, knowing he had only one shot left. Nebraska was hit, blood running from his mouth, head on one side, big body canted precariously. But he had palmed up his sixgun now and was raising it deliberately when Durango shot him through the head. The giant body made a mighty splash as it tumbled into the muddy waters.

⋆ ⋆ ⋆

It would be a long time before the floodwaters receded. The rivers' banks had collapsed and the watercourses were now joined, forming the wide lake.

Three days after the storm, Durango was standing on the stoop of Della's porch, left arm in a slim sling, smoking a cigarillo and staring out over miles of muddy water gleaming in limpid sunlight. Luckily, much of Della's land was not flooded.

'I don't think the railroad'll risk building here, Della. Even when the waters do run off, that part of the valley'll be prone to flooding whenever there's heavy rain. No railroad'll chance that.'

'No, I guess not.' She, like everyone else in the valley, was disappointed. 'According to Arlo — who's working at being sheriff again, despite Doc Mayfield ordering him to stay in bed — Dancey's plan was to drive out the homesteaders and then sell the abandoned land to the railroad: he was desperate for money after losing on his last trail drive because of low beef prices.'

'Just plain greedy, I reckon. But he had another string to his bow, too — he'd somehow figured out Case stole that gold from the Dakota mines' assay office.'

'He and Nebraska used to drink together a lot,' Della told him. 'Maybe something slipped out and Dancey noted it: he was very sly.'

Durango nodded. 'That could be it. Anyway, seems Case buried the gold on what was free range at the time, letting things cool down before he tried to use it, I suppose, but when the land was opened for homesteading, O'Hagen moved in and built his still right where the gold was hidden. Which kept Case from getting at it.'

Jason Case was badly wounded, still in the infirmary: it was not likely he would survive. Dying, and afraid to meet his Maker, he confessed to Doc Mayfield about the robbery. Dancey was dead, drowned, though Durango's bullet would've killed him in the end, anyway.

Brant Collier acted the innocent, claimed no knowledge of the wild goings-on in the valley. No one could effectively prove different now. (Some months later, it would be revealed that he had once been a bank manager in California and embezzled some funds. Under a new name, he came to Killdeer Valley, kept the money in his house, drawing on it as necessary. He didn't dare put it in a bank. The US marshals already had a warrant out for his arrest under his true name. And, inevitably, a marshal tracked him down to Killdeer Valley. By his scaly scalp and the special salve he needed . . .)

The surviving homesteaders and ranchers petitioned the territorial government to consider the feasibility of draining the valley or even turning the lake into a dam. Both would be expensive projects but after extensive lobbying, the politicians agreed to give the idea consideration.

'If they give it the OK, you'll be able to build up your spread to how you want it after all, Della,' Durango said after the news had come through. 'You're lucky here, with only a small area flooded.'

'I hope you're right.' She handed him

a cup of coffee. He took it awkwardly with his left hand, working it out of the sling first. He still didn't have full use of his fingers, spilled some, irritably changed the cup to his right hand.

'Damn! Doc says I'll get full feeling back eventually but meantime, if some flashy catches me with a glass of beer in my gun hand . . . ' He shrugged.

She frowned. 'Can't you change your way of life?'

'Not the kind of life you can retire from, Della — unless you're lying six feet under.'

'Oh, how can you joke about such things!' She was angry and it surprised him a little.

'If I start worrying about it, it'll get me killed.'

'I'm sorry, Durango, but it seems so stupid! Waiting for someone who's faster on the draw to show up one day and — and — ' She broke off, at a loss for words, her eyes glistening.

'I've known gunfighters try to retire, Della. It never stopped some fool tracking them down, and keep on crowding 'em until it just had to end in a gunfight.'

After a while she said hesitantly, 'On second thoughts, if it was me, I believe I'd take that chance, try to enjoy a little peace. Even if I knew it may not last forever.'

He gave her a steady look. 'Well, if I could find a place like Killdeer Valley, I might give it some thought.'

'Why go looking for somewhere *like* Killdeer Valley when you're already here? You have a place to stay, if you want. The flood waters'll go down eventually. You could even file on some of the land that's still for homesteading.'

'Be neighbours? You and me?'

She studied his sober face. 'Why not?'

'I guess it could be worth thinking about,' he said slowly, after a few moments.

She didn't answer but, as she cleared away the coffee things, she was singing softly to herself.

Other titles in the
Linford Western Library:

FIND MADIGAN!

Hank J. Kirby

Bronco Madigan was the top man in the US Marshals' Service — and now he was missing. Working on the most important and most dangerous mission he'd ever been assigned, he'd disappeared into the gunsmoke. Everything pointed to him being one of the many dead bodies left along the bloody trail. Even his sidekick, Kimble, was almost ready to give up the search, but the Chief's orders were very clear: 'Find Madigan . . . at all costs!'